Frandroisco,
I HOPE TH
LIFE, ALL Yc

. . . **LAUGHS LAST**

DYLAN BRODY

First Printing, 2013, Wheelman
Press

Second Printing, 2016, The Purveyor of Fine
Words and Phrases

Printed in the United States of America

A Purveyor of Fine Words and Phrases Publication

DEDICATION

This book is for my grandfather and for Carl Reiner who seem to merge into one person in my mind's eye.

ACKNOWLEDGEMENTS

This book would not have happened if not for Ann Patchett and David Sedaris, who inspire me with their work and honor me deeply by remembering who the hell I am.

It also comes out of my experiences with Steve Allen, who made me laugh aloud at the television when I was a child and gave me time when I was an adult, and George Carlin who gave me something to aspire to and encouragement at a moment when I most needed it. A debt of gratitude is also owed to Paul Provenza, who said exactly the things I needed to hear at exactly the moment I needed to hear them and then put them in writing for good measure.

CHAPTER ONE

1994

Damon tried not to dwell on the cardboard boxes. They made him feel melancholy at the exact moment that he wanted to exude energy and excitement. They made him nostalgic for times he would not have imagined remembering fondly as they occurred. The small one-bedroom apartment had been at various times a depressive's prison, a fortress of solitude, a pot-smoker's paradise and a writer's retreat. Now, the stained carpet, the packed boxes, the drifts of dust and lint in corners revealed by newly removed furniture turned the cramped intimacy of the living space into a warehouse for memories. Damon did not have time to absorb the wash of emotions. Damon had to get the refrigerator onto the hand truck and he had to do it while being cheerful and enthusiastic, so as to make the experience of helping him move pleasant for Cynthia and Matthew.

Cynthia steadied the hand truck. Damon pushed against the side of the refrigerator with his shoulder. Matthew pulled the pointy end of a pizza slice into his mouth and said, "Rock it. Don't lift it," although the words were muffled by the food.

"What does it look like I'm doing?" Damon asked, struggling for traction on the linoleum.

"I don't know. I'm not watching."

"You're also not helping much."

"I'm here in a supervisory capacity only."

"Then you oughta be watching," Damon said.

Cynthia laughed. Damon grunted, pushing. Matthew chewed. The phone rang.

"I thought that was already shut off," Cynthia said to Damon.

"I thought you unplugged it and packed it," Damon said to Matthew.

"You want me to get it?" Matthew asked.

"If it won't interfere with your supervisory duties, that'd be great."

Matthew grabbed the cordless receiver from the charging base. "You've reached the historical site of Damon Blazer's former apartment. For our hours of operation press one now. To reach the gift shop, press—Whoa. Whoa. Whoa. Stop pressing buttons. I was kidding. This is Matthew Grey speaking. Who's calling please?"

He turned to Damon, holding the phone between his ear and his shoulder so he'd be free to take another bite. "It's for you. It's an Alice Blazer. You want to talk to her?"

"Give me the phone, shmuck."

Matthew tossed the instrument without checking Damon's readiness. Damon caught it awkwardly and tossed a hostile look in return. "Hey, Mom," he said. "We're sort of in the middle here."

Then he heard the tone in his mother's voice.

1985

In his one-room apartment on West 17th Street, Damon had marked the floor with masking tape to show the location of the little span of sunlight that had appeared and then vanished at just after noon on January 8th. Apparently, the alignment of buildings across the street and beyond was such that they created something of a solar calendar. In the weeks since he had first seen the little slash of light, he had used small strips of tape to mark its shifting position, jotting times on them in pen to keep track of the sun's arrival and departure. He didn't yet know what he would do with this information, but he had a vague idea that he would eventually create some kind of conceptual art sundial on the floor.

He placed a square of tape to mark the point at which the sun had vanished on this day, checked the time on his plastic, digital watch, noted the numbers on the tape and reached for a bong hit. The phone rang.

"Telephone. Damon speaking," he said into the receiver.

His mother said, "Hi, Damon. I hope I'm not bothering you."

"No," he said. "I'm writing, but I can take a break."

"It's Poppa," his mother said.

Damon heard the tone in her voice, the sorrow, the worry, the tension. He knew already what it was that she was calling to say. He knew from those   two words why she had picked up the phone, why she had dialed. He knew that this was one in a series of difficult and uncomfortable calls, each one driving the pain a little deeper. Still, in his early twenties Damon had barely begun to control his Comedy Tourette's. Before he could think, before it could even occur to him to think, he said, "No it's not, Mom. I know your voice."

She paused for a moment, letting the quick rejoinder hang in a slow silence. Then she said, "Your grandfather died in his sleep last night and . . . You don't have to come to the funeral if you don't want to but—"

"Yeah, I do," Damon said.

"I know you and Poppa were close, Damon. But sometimes when you're around people you don't . . . well, you know what I mean."

"I made Poppa a promise, Mom. I have to go to the thing."

"You promised Poppa you'd go?"

"Yeah. Yeah, sort of. I promised him I'd do something for him."

Damon glanced at the small, crumpled brown paper bag atop the books on his milk-crates and salvage-boards bookcase.

"What?" His mother asked, suddenly confused. "When did you talk to Poppa?"

1982

Poppa pressed the brown paper bag into Damon's hand, crumpling the top half tightly as though the contents might try to escape were it not gripped shut. His hands were strong, even as he lay in the hospital bed recovering from that first heart attack. A tube across his upper lip fed oxygen into his nostrils. "You have to promise me," Poppa said. "You *have to!*

"You're not gonna die," Damon assured him. "Yeah, yeah. Maybe not now. But eventually I will. We both know that."

"Well, sure. Eventually."

"And you have to promise me. You have to promise me you'll do this."

"Really, Poppa? I mean, are you serious about this?"

"Did I ask you to come here?"

"Yeah."

"Did I pay for your airfare?"

"You bought me a train ticket."

"'Paid for your airfare' sounds better."

"Yeah."

"More generous."

"Fine. You paid my way here."

"I did that so I could give you this. So I could make you promise."

"If this is really what you want."

"It is. This is really what I want."

Poppa released the bag into Damon's hand, but he maintained eye contact for a long, hard time to be sure he'd driven the point home.

"Okay," Damon said. "I promise. But . . . why?" And at that question, Alvie Grunman grinned because he had been thinking about this for quite some time.

1985

"I made the promise a long time ago," Damon told his mother. "It doesn't matter. I made him a promise."

"All right. Well, I'll let you know when the service is all set up. And the burial. You know it has to be soon. Jewish law says—"

"Yeah. I know. I'll plan on traveling tomorrow."

He glanced at the masking-tape sundial on his floor, realizing he was going to miss at least a day, maybe two, of marking the sun's progress. On that day, February 23rd, it had lasted from twelve fourteen to one oh nine pm. Then his mother had called him and he had heard that tone in her voice.

1994

"Yeah," Damon said. "We've had this conversation before. I know about Jewish law."

Cynthia watched Damon carefully. So did Matthew, though it didn't stop him from reaching for another slice of pizza.

"Are you saying that you don't want me to come, Mom?"

His eyes were closed as he spoke on the phone now. He listened to the voice at the other end, the world at the other end. He imagined his mother standing beside the wall-mounted phone despite the long spiral cord that hung doubled nearly to the floor and could stretch far enough to sit at the kitchen table. He imagined her speaking into the phone he had used in childhood. He imagined her holding the receiver he had run to take from her or from Dad or from Leonard, sliding in his socks down the hard-wood hallway to the kitchen door, for his turn to talk when Poppa called.

"I—you know what? I didn't ask you what Leonard said. I can imagine what Leonard said. I asked if *you* want me to come. 'Cause if you don't want me there . . ."

Even without hearing the other end of the line, Cynthia could tell he had trailed off; he had not been interrupted. She knew him well enough for that. She knew that he was holding back responses. The Comedy Tourette's, he called it. He had thought of a joke, something funny, or just snide, and had chosen not to say it. Now, she knew, whatever his mother was saying, Damon could barely hear her. He was playing the line over and over in his head, trying to find his way back into the moment, trying to let go of the missed opportunity to get a laugh, even as he knew the line could not possibly have gotten a laugh. Those were the only times he was able to control the impulse at all. He could only control his tongue and keep the joke from emerging if the words could not possibly get a laugh because of the circumstance or the particular person to whom he had been about to speak.

"I would like to be there," he said. "But, again, that is not what I asked you."

The pause was sad and filled with hurtful things that might be said at the other end of the line and then Damon said, "I'll plan on flying tomorrow morning."

Thinking of the old, plastic receiver his mother would hang in the metal cradle on the kitchen wall, Damon pressed the button that disconnected his cordless line and tossed it back to Matthew who snagged it from the air, while turning his body to protect the half-consumed slice in his other hand. He returned the phone to its charging station.

Cynthia and Matthew said nothing for a moment, waiting for Damon to say something, to report fully on the conversation. He said, "Don't just hang that up, Matt. Unplug it and put it in one of the boxes."

He looked around at the boxes now, taking them in, nondescript brown cubes full of belongings that meant nothing. Still, somehow it seemed each one held a straining clutter of poorly-packed memories, ready to explode into the room if the interlocked flaps were just pulled apart to release them. He turned back to the refrigerator and put his shoulder against it. "Hold that thing steady," he said to Cynthia as he started again to rock the appliance forward, walking it an inch at a time toward the leading edge of the hand truck.

"Are you okay?" She asked.

"Me? I'm fine. My father is dead. My brother is bitter and angry and doesn't want me at the funeral. My mother is afraid she agrees with him. But me? I've never been better."

And then he bent down to see if he could make better progress by lifting the refrigerator instead of rocking it.

CHAPTER TWO

1994

The drizzle hit the windshield and crawled upward, propelled by the wind of freeway speed. Each drop left a lazy snail-trail reaching up toward the roof of the car. Damon stared dully at the Sunday light traffic of the 405, leaving the effort of focus to Cynthia.

His right index finger throbbed warmly, protected in a metal and foam pharmacy splint. He had taken a Vicodin left over from a wisdom tooth extraction of years gone by, but now he wondered if age had rendered the pill ineffectual. He also wondered if he should have packed the few remaining pills to take with him on the trip.

A pickup truck sped past on the right, throwing a bucket of water up against the window next to his ear. Damon jumped, startled by the sound, and then chuckled at his own jumpiness.

"You're stoned out of your mind," Cynthia said.

"I'm drugged out of my mind," Damon said. "There's a difference."

Cynthia nodded. "Is it helping any?"

Damon held up his injured finger and tapped it lightly against the window glass. "Yeah. Distant throbbing, but that's about it."

"You're going to sleep through the whole flight, aren't you?"

"I hope so."

The car slowed a bit as the freeway became more crowded four exits before the airport. There was no time on any day that the freeway did not become more crowded four exits before the airport.

"Is it going to be okay with you if I start unpacking your stuff while you're away?"

"Are you kidding me? I scheduled my father's death to avoid dealing with that."

Cynthia nodded but did not manage the obligatory chuckle. Knowing that he would be looking for the laugh, she glanced back over her shoulder and made an unnecessary lane change to create the illusion that she had just been distracted and had missed the joke.

"Okay," she said. "I'll get you as settled as I can before you're back."

"Be my guest," he said.

"Not anymore," she said and squeezed his leg.

"Yeah. That'll be good."

They moved along like that, with her hand on his knee as she drove, comforting. The traffic remained dense. The conversation and the rain remained scattered.

"You're sure you don't want me to come?" she asked.

"Yeah. I can do this alone," he said.

Had circumstances allowed, they'd have spent the day together unpacking boxes in their new apartment, laughing about things they had packed to bring that should clearly have been thrown away, enjoying the shared anticipation of their new life in a shared home. Instead, they drove in near silence, trading intermittent half-sentences.

Each of them thought about their new life as they drove, the shared apartment, but both felt wrong to be thinking about such a thing at this moment. Cynthia imagined a future that felt like family, that felt like marriage. She imagined sitting near one another, each reading a book they'd heard about recently on NPR. She imagined making breakfast in the kitchen and feeling very wifely as she brought the food out on plates to eat with him on a small dining table in the proper area of the big living room/dining room space. She imagined calling out to him that breakfast was ready and seeing him come in from the second bedroom, which they had designated as their shared office. She imagined working in that office together, imagined him clacking away at the keyboard of his computer, feet up on his desk, plastic keyboard in his lap, as she wrote up lesson plans and cut out the laminated shapes from a big sheet that she would use to teach the kids about squares and rectangles and circles. She did not say any of this because she knew Damon was about to fly East to see his family, to attend his father's funeral. She knew he was in pain and drugged against the pain, that he was sad and anxious. She knew that he was grieving for the loss of a man whom he had loved deeply, if not purely; well, if not perfectly. She was fairly certain that such a state would be nearly incompatible with her forward-looking, excited fantasy life just now.

Damon imagined their new life as well. He imagined that they would get a dog. He imagined sleeping on the sofa in their living room, feeling the warm sunlight on his face and the warm dog on his feet. He imagined sitting at the computer in their shared office, hearing the dog on the floor nearby snuffling and snoring softly. He imagined pretending to be focused on his work, tapping away at the keyboard while he surreptitiously watched Cynthia write big careful letters on a wide sheet of poster board for her classroom. He imagined the easy beauty of her face when she focused on the task, her feet folded up under her in the chair, leaning forward on her elbows as if she were, herself, one of her kindergarten students, involved in an art project just a little bit challenging for such small unpracticed hands. He imagined lingering at the refrigerator in their little kitchen, watching her rinse off a plate, the warm, clear water running over her small hands. He wondered for perhaps the thousandth time since he'd met her, why she did so much more actual work than he did and yet always seemed to have cleaner fingernails and undamaged cuticles. He said only, "You know, you put the cute in cuticles," but without the drowsy drugged thought process that got him there, it seemed an odd non sequitur as they pulled onto the roadway marked "Departures."

Cynthia chuckled and said, "That's funny. Sweet. You have to find a place to use that."

"I thought I just had."

Then, they pulled up to the curb. With a sharp pain in his broken finger, Damon pulled his bag out of the trunk. Cynthia's taillights moved away from him into the flow of drizzle-touched travel traffic. He stood for longer than he might have had there been no Vicodin, watching her go.

1992

In June of 1992 a sudden thunderstorm that none of the local weatherpersons had predicted interrupted, but did not correct a drought. Damon, walking back to his car, saw the lightning divide the night sky and felt the thunder crack across his belly, the way one feels the drum line as a parade passes by. As the heavy drops pelted him, he turned off the sidewalk, slipping inside the weeknight emptiness of an independent coffee house. He approached the counter where the only on-duty employee stood, reading a paperback book. She glanced up at him, saw that he was studying the chalk-written menu and went back to reading. After a minute he said, "Can I just get a coffee?"

She looked up from the book, blinked, and then said, "Sure." She chuckled as she turned to pour him the requested cup.

"That's funny?" he asked.

"It's funny that you walked into a coffee house, studied the menu, and then that was your order."

"Wow. Mockery. Nice." He watched her pour his coffee as he dragged his wallet out of a pocket. She had small hands and startlingly clean, unpolished fingernails. Suddenly, he did not want the conversation to end when he handed her the bills, when she gave him the proper change. He said, "Have you seen it out there?"

"No," she said. "Born and raised in here at Avajay."

He chuckled, handing her money.

"You're an easy laugh." She returned his change.

"Not usually," he said. "You're funny."

She shrugged. He stood for a moment, searching for something more to say before sitting down to drink coffee and hope for a break in the rain. Her focus went back to her book, a well-worn copy of <u>Raise High the Roofbeam, Carpenters</u> and <u>Seymour: An Introduction</u>. It was one he hadn't read, though he had heard the title. He did not want to start a conversation by telling her that. He wanted her attention again, though. He wanted her to look up at him, to smile, to chuckle at his foolishness, his awkwardness. He wanted to hear her startlingly casual snideness, the way it came with a sly smile of shared naughtiness, an acknowledgement that it was not appropriate. He wanted to see her eyes, to memorize the way their wolfish brown seemed a little bit glowing under her dark eyebrows.

The moment had already lasted too long. He had outwaited the possibility of light timing. He wanted to have responded with a witty rejoinder to everything she'd said thus far. He wanted to already be bantering comfortably with her, but instead he stood in silence holding, but not sipping his coffee, watching her read.

He said, "Comedy Tourette's."

"What?" she asked.

"I have it too. The inability to keep from blurting out the punch line when I hear a set-up."

"Really?" she said. "I hadn't noticed that about you so much."

Had he not been so happy to have her looking at

him again, to have her talking to him again, he might have felt foolish or defensive. He did not. He felt only that everything was going to be okay as long as this woman kept conversing with him. "I might be a little off my game," he told her.

"Why's that?"

He didn't want to tell her that it was because she was very, very pretty. He didn't want to sound like an adolescent, professing his sudden belief in love at first sight. His mind raced through things he did not want to say. It raced and raced and raced as time slowed around him and at last he said, "I haven't read that one. I know the title, but I haven't read it."

"Salinger," she informed him.

"Yeah. I read Catcher in the Rye in high school."

"I didn't get that. I think it's too male. But this one I've read four or five times. And Franny and Zooey."

"I read the stories. I liked the stories."

Then she really studied him for a moment, he made eye contact. He hoped that whatever she was scrutinizing him to find, he was proving sufficient. Needing to hide just a little bit, he sipped his coffee at last. Then he said, "I'm Damon."

She told him her name was Cynthia.

1994

Damon stood, watching the tail end of her car slide off along the airport roadway. It seemed even her car had a sexy walk as it moved away. He could still feel the remnants of her Chapstick on his lips, left behind by the goodbye kiss. He could still feel her weight and her warmth against his body, a ghost of a hug that he might have carried away unconsciously had it not been for the drowsy, dreamlike perspective offered by the pain killer.

He felt suddenly very alone and very young in the span of time between being left here by Cynthia and the time he would be spending with his family. What was left of it. His mother. His brother. He sighed.

The car was gone now, and still he stood, staring in the direction it had gone. The throbbing in his finger was a distant thing, a warm reminder that he was injured. He lifted his bag with his uninjured hand and slung it over a shoulder. *Apparently,* he thought, *the expiration date on Vicodin is not sacrosanct.*

CHAPTER THREE

1994

Damon climbed into Leonard's car. He had to turn and squeeze his bag between the seats to push it into the back. Leonard had not popped the trunk for him, had not stepped out of the car into the cool autumn air to offer a hand.

Damon asked, "Where's mom?"

"Where do you think she is, Damon?" Leonard responded gruffly. "She's at home, crying. What're you? Upset 'cause your Mommy didn't pick you up at the airport?"

"Just a question, Leonard," Damon said, but in truth he was disappointed. He had assumed his mother would pick him up. He wanted the comfort of his mother, even with all their disagreements and tensions. It had not occurred to him that Leonard might come; certainly not that Leonard might come alone.

A shuttle van pulled up to the curb directly in front of them, making it impossible for Leonard to pull forward immediately. To back up and make space to drive around the van, Leonard turned toward Damon, twisting to see through the rear windshield. As his brother turned, Damon flinched away. Damon felt a wave of shame, a wave of hatred toward his brother, and a wash of self-loathing all at once. Leonard laughed.

1985

Damon lay in the snow outside the synagogue, only vaguely aware of the people emerging, returning to their cars. Some of them turned to stare. Others did not notice at all, wrapped up in their own conversations, their own grief, some still chuckling quietly to themselves. Damon heard those chuckles clearly despite all that was demanding his attention at that moment, Leonard's knee on his chest, the bare fists that kept crunching against his face. He knew that those same chuckles were clear to Leonard, enraging him as much as they comforted Damon.

"You. Little. Fuck," Leonard said, punctuating his words with blows. "What the fuck is wrong with you?"

Damon wondered if his nose was bleeding or if there was just some snow melting down his upper lip. "Wrong with me?" he said. "I'm not the one kicking the crap out of someone at a funeral."

"You little fucking—" Damon was no longer listening. At twenty-one he liked to think of himself as a grown man, but just now he did not feel like a grown man. He was a little boy, misunderstood and bullied. He felt weak and foolish. He knew he could have avoided this. He knew before he did it, maybe not that he'd be beaten senseless in a snow bank, but that nobody would really understand. Nobody but him. He knew that was why the task had been given to him, too. Suddenly, it was all very clear to him just how well he had understood his grandfather. It was very clear to him just how well his grandfather had understood him. It was very clear to him just how great a presence Poppa had been in his life and how little he had availed himself of that presence. He wished he had known before. He wished he had visited the old man more often in the years of his declining health, that he had spent every weekend listening to the old stories, learning the old jokes. He really knew so little of Poppa's life, the years on the road, working with his wife on stages across the country. He knew Poppa had been on TV once or twice, but he didn't know when or on what shows. He had learned so much from his grandfather, but he had learned so little about him. If he had visited more often, perhaps it might have occurred to ask Poppa about himself, about his history, about his life with Trixie. If he had been willing to bear the pain of seeing Poppa weakened and waning, the old man might have loosened his grip on the purse strings of his own memory and offered Damon insight into his history, insight that went deeper than comedic craft and the navigation of the humorscape.

Damon stopped struggling and let the blows come, one after another, as punishment for those mistakes, not for the day's events, not as punishment for what Leonard thought he had done wrong. He let the blows come as punishment for his own weakness, his own pathetic inability to confront pain.

1976

Damon sat on the steps of the house in Turdoc, New Jersey, watching Leonard and his friends push one another jovially and make jokes at the expense of classmates who were not present. He pretended to read a Robert Heinlein book that he had checked out of the school library, but he was watching. Autumn came to Turdoc with a rush of brightly colored maple leaves and a chill wind that promised snow for weeks before it finally drifted down. He pulled his jacket around himself and resented Leonard for having so many friends, for being able to push them jovially. He resented Leonard for saying, "Do whatever you want, but you're not hanging out with us." He resented Leonard for having mediocre grades and no allergies.

One of Leonard's friends told an idiotic joke that hinged on a large-breasted woman uttering what could only be described as a single entendre. Damon found himself silently rewording it so that it would make sense as an actual joke, while Leonard's friends laughed. He guessed, correctly, that his revision was far closer to the joke the kid had heard than it was to the joke the kid had told.

Damon was never able to understand why people laughed at jokes that weren't funny. At twelve years old, he had already spent hours at the phonograph, listening to George Carlin, to Bob Newhart, to Bill Cosby. He had listened and memorized. He had dissected and re-examined. He loved the sound of their voices, the rhythms, the structures, the carefully worded sentences that took the audience in one di- rection and then pulled them back on themselves. Those were jokes he could understand, even when he didn't fully comprehend their significance. The bad jokes told in the lunch room, though, held nothing for him, no wit, no sparkle.

Leonard said loudly, "I got one! I got one! Why did the chicken cross the road?"

Before he had time to think about consequences, before he had time to realize there were consequences to be considered, Damon said, "To avoid hearing a crappy joke?"

The boys around Leonard laughed, surprised by the unexpected answer that had come from the house's front steps, from the younger boy who seemed to be engrossed in his book. Damon reveled in the laughter and pretended to continue reading, continued to pretend. That was the secret, Poppa had told him. "Never check for the audience's reaction. You have something more important to do than get the laugh," he had said. "Let them have the laugh to themselves."

Leonard looked at him hard as the boys around him laughed. One of the boys shoved Leonard. It was friendly, but as he did it he said, "Ooooh, Leonard. *Burn.*"

Leonard said, "Where'd you get that, Damon? One of your records?"

Damon looked up at him, now. Damon did not like being accused of stealing the joke from a record. Damon had not stolen a joke from a record in two years and he would never do so again.

1974

At the breakfast table, Damon cut a syrup-soaked toaster waffle with his fork. Poppa sat next to him smoking a cigar, his first of the day. Poppa was visiting for a week, while new floors were put in at his house in upstate New York. Damon's mother stood at the counter, putting sandwiches in bags for him and Leonard. Leonard was upstairs somewhere and Dad was working on the New York Times crossword puzzle with a cigarette burning in the ashtray near his left hand, the hand in which he held his pen. Without looking up from the food, Damon said, "You know what's an oxymoron? Jumbo shrimp. Also, Military intelligence."

Poppa laughed aloud. Mom laughed a hissing little laugh. Dad looked up from the puzzle sharply and said, "That's not yours."

"How do you know?" Damon asked.

"Simon," Poppa scolded. "You don't accuse someone of—" but Dad cut him off.

"You're nine, Damon. Do you know what 'oxymoron' means?"

"It means—um—" Damon squirmed, trying to find the meaning that would make sense of the laugh he had heard the joke get.

Before he could get there, Poppa stepped in. He had never heard his grandfather sound so worried, so angry. "Is that true, Damon? Where did you get that joke?"

Damon was confused. People told jokes they had

heard all the time. "I heard one," they would say. Or, "Have you heard the one about the two peanuts walking through the park?" Damon said, "I heard it last night. George Carlin said it. On Flip Wilson."

Dad nodded with satisfaction and wrote in a five-letter word on the puzzle.

"That's no good," Poppa said sternly. "You don't use other people's material."

"I don't see what you're so upset about—" Damon started.

Poppa said, very seriously, "You listen to me, Damon. Civilians tell jokes they've heard. And some of those jokes are good. You learn them, you tell them, it's fine. That's not the same thing as material. You hear a comic tell a joke, or a comedian, that's their livelihood. That's their life. That's their blood. Sometimes, the only thing they really own in the world is their jokes and the only thing they'll leave behind is the laughs. Do you understand what I'm telling you?"

Damon only vaguely understood what Poppa was telling him. He said, "Don't do jokes I heard on TV?"

"Good enough for now!" Poppa announced. He smacked the table with his hand like an auctioneer accepting a final bid.

As Damon chewed his waffle, he felt his grandfather's eyes on him and he felt a deep, sad shame for what he had done, although he didn't really understand why. He also felt that he had just learned something very, very important, although he hadn't yet. That would not happen for another three minutes.

1976

Damon met his brother's gaze now, aware of the other boys watching, waiting. Leonard had meant to shut him down. Leonard had meant the barb as a mean jab that would silence Damon, make him feel small for being funny, for caring about the things he cared about, for speaking up and getting a laugh from the boys who were Leonard's friends, not his. Damon did not hear it that way. Damon heard it as an attack, but also as a challenge. He heard the hostility, the sharpness, but he also heard the absurdity of the accusation. He said, "That's right, Lenny. I stole that joke from National Lampoon's Big Album of Why Did the Chicken Cross the Road Jokes."

The boys all laughed again. Damon could not stop himself from driving the point home. "It's sold a million copies, Len. Mostly to five-year-olds, but it's good that you're still getting your money's worth out of it."

Now Leonard's friends were laughing so hard that it was hard for Damon not to smile at them in gratitude, but he knew better. This only stayed funny as long as it seemed like they were really mad at one another. Leonard was doing his part perfectly. He was working the straight man's slow burn like a professional. Damon had never felt closer to him than at this moment.

Leonard said, "Oh, I bet you got a million of these. Huh?"

"Sure," Damon said. "I got a great knock knock

joke. You wanna hear it?"

"Fuck you," Leonard said.

Leonard's friends said, "Do it!" and "What's the joke?"

"Knock knock," Damon offered.

"Who's there?" three of the boys asked, overlapping one another to be part of the show.

"Lenny," Damon answered.

Leonard glared. Nobody said anything. Then Leonard, very quietly, very dangerously said, "Lenny who?"

Damon said, "Lenny think for an hour or two and maybe I'll come up with something funny to say."

The boys howled as Leonard lifted Damon from the steps and threw him hard to the pavement. His right fist crossed Damon's jaw twice before it dawned on him that Leonard hadn't been playing his part brilliantly. Leonard wasn't a straight man at all. He was a civilian.

Even as he took the beating, felt the blood flow from his nose, felt his lip tear open against his own tooth, he felt sorry. He was not as bothered by the beating as he was by the knowledge that he had brought it on himself. He had made his brother look foolish. No. No, he had meant to do that. The problem wasn't that he had made him look foolish. He felt awful because he had made his brother *feel* foolish. It was his older brother, just talking to his friends, telling normal jokes badly like normal people do and he had stepped in and made him feel like an idiot. He had been a bully. He didn't mean to be a bully. He didn't want to be a bully.

Lenny punched him a last time and then   leaned

close to his face and said, "Not so funny now, huh, Damon?"

Damon agreed with him. He didn't feel funny at all.

1985

The blows stopped abruptly and it took Damon a moment to get his bearings. He realized he had momentarily lost consciousness. Fragments of memory scattered around him like the melting shards of a dream after a midday nap. He had been talking to Poppa. He had been a child. He couldn't remember all the bits and pieces. The snow near his face was pink and he realized that his own blood was causing the color at the same time that he knew he hadn't lost enough blood to turn it a shocking red.

He rolled to his back and then groaned to his feet to find his father holding Leonard in a half-nelson and scolding him. "What's the matter with you?" Dad was saying. "Your mother just lost her father today and now she has to see this?"

"Dad," Leonard whined, suddenly a child in a grown-man's overcoat. "What're you picking on me for? You saw what he did in there."

Damon waited for it. This was the moment. He was bleeding on the ground, but this would be the moment of victory. His father would understand, would come to his defense, and would explain the bond he'd had with Poppa, the reason for what he'd done.

"Yeah. I saw. And there's no excuse for that non-sense, either. But Damon can't help it. You know that. He's always been like this. You should know better."

Damon, lying on his back in the blood stained snow, felt dizzy for a moment. He felt himself reeling at last from all the blows. Then he knew, with an absolute certainty, that only he knew why he had done what he had done. Only he had known of the promise he'd made. Only he had carried out his grandfather's wishes. He had to carry the burden of honoring his grandfather on his own. The responsibility was his, and the consequences were his. He had done the right thing. He knew that. Regardless of what his brother thought, regardless of what his father thought, regardless even of pain he might have caused his mother on that day, he had done the right thing.

He stood up, shaky and hurt but feeling, for all his weakness, as though he had just been bar mitzvahed. "Now," he thought to himself, "I am a man."

He brushed snow from his coat. He wiped blood from his face. He moved with his family toward the car.

He checked his jaw and his ribs for cracks, knowing that there were none. He heard people getting into their cars. Some of them were still chuckling and he allowed himself to enjoy that sound, even as he felt guilty for enjoying the anger he knew it must still be triggering in Leonard.

He did not know, in that moment, that they had not yet gotten to the most awkward part of the funeral.

1994

"Oh, come on," his older brother said.

"You really think that's hilarious, don't you, Leonard?"

"I look back for traffic and you flinch like a school girl? That's funnier than all that shit you do in your act." Something in his tone put ugly finger quotes around the word "act."

"Yeah," Damon said, "There's nothing funnier than hitting someone until they fear your every move."

"You're such a baby," Leonard said.

Damon pulled his small notebook out of his pocket and made a note to himself to write jokes about the way in which families revert to ancient patterns when they come together. In parentheses he noted, "Aging uncles giving one another titty-twisters." He knew that would be enough for him to remember the side images that had occurred to him of Aunt Sadie enduring a swirly in the bathroom during Thanksgiving dinner. He also knew it would be the opportunity he'd been looking for to refer to her in his act as "my miniature Aunt Sadie," a phrase that had been getting conversational laughs for years but had yet to find its way on stage.

"What're you writing?" Leonard asked. A hint of nervousness edged his tone. He pulled out of the airport and onto the access road that would take him to the highway.

"An idea for a bit. Don't worry about it."

"That's not what I'm worried about," Leonard said.

"Yeah?"

"Yeah. Listen. I don't want you to– you know– do anything stupid."

"Oh, for Christ's sake, Leonard."

"I'm serious. You fucked up Poppa's funeral. You know that. That was completely ridiculous, what you did."

"I didn't fuck up Poppa's funeral."

"People were laughing, Damon. Mom was crying her eyes out, and people were laughing."

"Yes. Yes, they were."

"That's fucked up."

Damon said nothing. He watched the woods slide by the side of the road, the forested stretches that very much did not line the byways of Los Angeles. He took in the rich, loamy color palate of the coast on which he grew up.

"You pull any of that shit at Dad's funeral and I will kick your ass."

"Well, that'll certainly open a new chapter in our relationship," Damon said. Then, "Oh. Wait. No. We've read that chapter before."

Leonard pulled the car onto the gravel shoulder and came to an abrupt stop on the side of the road. He turned so that he could more easily point a finger in Damon's face. "I am not kidding, you little fuck. Listen to me. Mom lost her husband. I lost my father. I don't know what your goddamn problem is with be-having like a normal fucking human being, but if you pull any of your stupid, 'Hey, everybody look at me' shit this time around, I am going to leave you so fucking battered you're going to have to do jokes about your looks when you get on Letterman. And this time you're not gonna have your Daddy to pull me off of you. You understand me? Is that clear enough?"

Damon said nothing. He stared out through the window as though the woods were still sliding by.

"What? No funny joke? No witty line to throw at me?"

Damon had several. He said none of them.

Lenny pulled back onto the road. Damon seethed in silence.

CHAPTER FOUR

1994

Damon stopped at the end of the walkway. He took a long, slow breath before taking those last few steps to the front door. He believed he was preparing himself, preparing himself to lift his bag up those stairs, preparing himself to return to the home that had housed his childhood, preparing himself to be of comfort and support to his grieving mother. None of these was true. He was really just looking at the steps.

He had sat on those steps so many times. He knew the sensation of them against his flesh. He knew their hardness. He knew the textured striations of the wood. He knew how ants moved up the risers and across the treads in the summertime and how the ice coated them in winter.

He had a dim memory, from long ago, from very early in his childhood, of his father replacing the tread of the last step before the small porch. He could see the hammer swinging down, pounding in a nail. He could smell the paint Dad had used to make that step look just like the others.

He let the breath out on a sigh and stepped forward.

1985

Damon sat on the steps the way he used to sit on the steps in childhood. It was too cold to sit outdoors, really, and he'd already spent too long outdoors today. Much too long. Still. He sat on the steps and felt the cold hard surface beneath him.

He kept his hands stuffed into his pockets. Each breath hung in the air in front of him as a cloud for a moment before vanishing.

He imagined himself fighting back against Leonard's onslaught, fighting like a character in a comic book. He imagined delivering arcing punches, all of his body weight behind two knuckles. He imagined Leonard's head snapping to the side with the impact, his shoulders following, his feet lifting off the ground just a little bit.

That was not all he imagined.

He imagined himself outside the synagogue as the blows came; saying something incredibly funny, something so incisive that even those who had been watching him get hit couldn't help but admire him for his wit and his composure. He couldn't find the right words, so he indulged in the fantasy of the moment after he spoke, the moment when he got the laugh and Leonard, fist raised, rage on his face, simply looked foolish.

He heard the squeak of the door behind him and did not turn to see who it was. If it was Leonard, he did not want to look nervous about being approached from behind. If it was Mom or Dad he had nothing to be nervous about. It wouldn't be Poppa. Poppa was gone.

The gentle closing of the door told him it was Dad who had come outside. There was a long silence. He could feel his father behind him, trying to decide what to say or perhaps just how to say whatever it was that he had decided to say.

Damon was angry. He was angry at his father for failing to fully take his side. He was angry at his father for not understanding the reason for what he had done. He was angry at his father for protecting him physically without defending his actions. He was angry that he needed his father's protection. He was angry that he was a grown man and he still could not defend himself against Leonard's barbarism.

Dad sat down next to him on the steps. They sat in silence for a time, their breath clouding and vanishing, clouding and vanishing.

"It's pretty cold out here," Simon said. He tried to sound casual, conversational, and not at all parental.

"Yeah," Damon said.

Their breath clouded and vanished.

"What're you thinking about?"

"Superpowers."

Dad snorted a little laugh, a laugh that said, "Of course," and "At your age?" and "That's amusingly honest," all at the same time.

Damon said, "Leonard's an asshole."

Dad shrugged his shoulders lightly. "Maybe," he said.

"He beat me up outside Poppa's funeral, Dad. How is that 'maybe?'"

"Leonard was angry, Damon. Your mother was crying. People were laughing. He didn't know how to protect her. And, frankly, he is just as certain that you're an asshole as you are that he is."

"Well then, I suppose it's okay that he beat the crap out of me." Damon put his hand on the step's tread to feel the wood grain, but his fingers found only a smooth coating of ice. He brushed the cold surface with his fingertips until it became moist.

"No. That wasn't okay."

"Did you tell him that?"

"Did I tell him that? Damon, you two are grown men. I can't tell you what to do anymore and I can't tell him what to do anymore."

"I see."

"Do you?" Dad said.

1972

Damon sat on the steps in the warm breeze of spring, the breeze that promised an end to school and the start of summer. The very last patches of snow still clung to the brown grass in the shaded spots, but even that was sickly gray, facing its last moments.

He rolled his Captain America comic book into a tube and looked through it at the houses across the street, focusing on windows, pretending it was a telescope. He looked at the windows without the tube and then with the tube again, trying to decide whether they were actually enlarged any by the imposed tunnel vision or just seemed that way by virtue of isolation.

The door opened behind him and he heard his

father emerge. Still looking out through the tube, he thought about how he knew that it was his father. Could he smell him? Was it the weight of his footsteps on the porch, the way he closed the door? He thought about the things one knows without knowing how one knows them.

Damon's father sat down beside him on the steps and looked out at the street.

After a minute or two of silence he said, "What are we looking at?"

"I'm just thinking," Damon said.

"You've been out here a while," Dad said.

"Yeah," Damon confirmed. Then he said, "Do you think you can ever figure out what's going to happen next just by knowing what happened last?"

"What do you mean?"

"Well . . ." Damon struggled to find language for complex thoughts that had been playing through his head. "Just now, when you came out, I didn't look, but I knew it was you. You know?"

"Okay."

"And I saw on TV where a guy got hypnotized and then he could remember things he didn't know he remembered."

"What kind of things?"

"A license plate number that he had only seen for a second. What color another guy's coat was. He was a witness and the cops needed stuff that he didn't remember."

"I see."

"So, I was thinking, maybe, if I got hypnotized so that I could figure stuff out without worrying about . . . I don't know . . . without worrying about how I knew it, I could take everything that I know   about what's happening right now and figure out what's going to happen in the future."

Dad laughed a snorting little laugh that said, "That's some pretty heady stuff for a kid your age," and "I think that's a little bit silly," and also, "Really? That's what you think about when you sit out here alone with a comic book?" Then he said, "So, you're thinking that the only thing that keeps people from knowing the future is a lack of hypnosis?"

Damon laughed. "No. Sort of. Just, maybe we all know more than we think we know. Maybe we all have a little bit of ability to see the future, we just don't trust it. Maybe there's a— I don't know— a pattern to everything that happens and the order it happens in."

"Damon," Dad said, stalling while he chose his words, "there's no such thing as super heroes."

"Who said anything about super heroes?"

"Prescience. Hypnosis that lets you see the future. Don't pretend that's not what you were talking about."

Dad took the rolled up comic book from his hand and looked through it himself, taking in bits of the world across the street through the four-color, glossy coated tube.

Damon felt his own eyebrows pulling down and inward. He didn't like it when his father did this, stating aloud the thing that he was trying to talk around. At the same time, it was comforting. His father had a special talent for ignoring the words and hearing what was behind them.

"Poppa says that everybody has a destiny."

"Yeah," Dad said. "Poppa also says that the Marx Brothers were more important to human history than The Manhattan Project."

"I don't know what that is."

"Your mother's father sees the world through a particular lens," Dad said. "He's a peculiar man."

"I like him a lot."

"I know you do, kiddo. But don't let him be your only influence. Okay?"

"You don't believe in destiny, do you?"

"No."

"What do you believe in?"

That seemed to be a difficult question. Dad tapped gently on the side of his own head with the rolled up comic book. He did this for a long time. Then he said, "I believe in fulfilling responsibilities. I believe in keeping promises and being a decent human being." Something in his inflection said that he wasn't done yet, so Damon held off on his next question, giving his father time to say, "I believe that the truth is of greater value than any individual's convenience."

"I think you're going to have to explain that one," Damon said. His father took a long breath, pulling the cool, moist spring air into his lungs while he tried to figure out how to explain the inherent value of objective truths to an eight-year-old with the vocabulary and comprehension of an eleven-year-old.

1985

"Yeah," Damon said to his father. "I understand completely. You think Leonard had a perfectly good reason to hit me, you just don't like that he actually did it."

Dad sighed. "Damon, you did what you did. Leonard did what Leonard did. I don't approve of any of it. I think you're too old to be pulling school-boy pranks and I think he's too old to be bullying you."

"Same old crap, huh Dad?" Damon let the ice melt gently, coldly under his fingertips until he reached the familiar texture of wood grain underneath.

"What do you mean?"

"When I came to you in grade school 'cause the kids in gym were beating me up in the locker room, do you remember what you said?"

"I can probably guess."

"I asked you why they hated me so much and you said that they didn't hate me. They resented me. You said they were jealous of me for my intelligence and my wit, for skipping a grade, for my ability to make the teachers laugh, for my nonviolent relationship with my parents. You remember this?"

"No."

"We were sitting right here on these steps. You know what you didn't bother to explain to me, Dad?"

"I'm sure you're going to tell me."

"You didn't explain to me that it wouldn't help to tell the other kids all of that. You know what doesn't stop a bully from hitting you? On-the-spot psychoanalysis."

Dad snorted. It was a snort that said, "I get that entirely," and also, "That's funny enough that you might be able to use it on stage," as well as, "I'm sorry I failed you as a father."

"When a child says he's being bullied, he wants protection. Not insight."

"You're not a child anymore, Damon. What does an adult want when he's being bullied? 'Cause I pulled your brother off of you today."

Damon had to think about that a bit. He circled his fingers in the cold, cold pool of water on the surface of the step. He shrugged. "You got any insight?"

"Yeah," Dad said. "But you're not going to like it."

"What've you got?"

"Only this. No matter who it is, no matter what they do, the hell of it is, they have their reasons."

Suddenly, Damon wished his father would go back inside. He had an eighth of an ounce of grass in a baggie in his pocket and he very much wanted to load up a bowl and put a little bit of distance between himself and the day's events.

1994

Damon climbed the steps into the house. He felt the familiar give and groan of the treads beneath his feet.

Leonard held the door open for him and he passed inside to the smell of stale cigarette smoke and fried food, which had so permeated his youth that even now he could not fully recognize the smell as anything other than a neutral odor of childhood, a safe smell of home.

CHAPTER FIVE

1994

Alice Blazer sat at the kitchen table with a glass of scotch. A cigarette burned in the ashtray. Hugs had already been exchanged, the bag taken upstairs to the guest room, the same room he had shared in childhood with Leonard, only now the bunk bed was gone, the posters, the blue ribbons for science projects, certificates of achievement for writing contests, Leonard's trophies for baseball and wrestling. Offers of food had been declined on the pretense that he was not hungry, although in fact he was a little noshy. He just didn't want his mother to start moving about the kitchen, clattering utensils and being a dutiful mother just now. He wanted to sit still and have her sit still and feel the warmth of the small kitchen around them.

Leonard had put a sporting event on the TV in the other room and the distant drone of the color commentators seeped in, occasionally punctuated by a grunt of reaction from the live viewer. He had excused himself, "Just to check the score, real quick," but Damon had seen his mother wince at the sound when Leonard squeaked into the groaning leather of their father's recliner and then worked the mechanism to lean back. "And that," Damon said, "is why they call him Captain Sensitivity."

His mother let out a laugh that came in a series

of hisses and gently slapped his wrist for mocking his brother, who was not in the room to defend himself.

"How're you holding up?" he asked her.

"I'm okay," she said. "Tired. I didn't sleep right."

"I can imagine."

"Had a little bit of heartburn. Kept being afraid it was chest pains."

Damon nodded.

"That's what he said yesterday morning. He said, 'It's probably just heartburn.' He took Tums."

Damon nodded.

"If I'd taken him to the hospital then . . ."

"When he said he had heartburn and took Tums? Why would you take him to the hospital for that?"

"He never got heartburn. We had the Tums for me."

"Still."

She sipped scotch. She took a long, last pull on the cigarette and then stubbed it out in the ashtray. She said, "Don't tell me I should quit. I don't need to hear that today."

"I didn't," Damon said. "I wasn't."

1992

Damon watched his mother gesture with the lit cigarette. He waited for her to say something. Finally he pulled a bag of grass out of his jacket pocket and began rolling a joint.

"Oh, Damon. I wish you wouldn't smoke that

stuff," his mother said.

"I wish you wouldn't smoke that stuff," he countered. He lit the joint and they sat together in the kitchen, each releasing smoke into the air with every second or third breath.

"She's very funny," he said.

Mom hissed a series of short, sharp hisses. "What?" Damon asked. "Why is that funny?"

"Just that 'funny' seems to be the most important thing to you. Again."

"Always," Damon said. Then he said, "You know what your father used to say."

"Yeah. Yeah, I do."

They sat together, smoking.

"Do you know if she wants children?"

"We've talked about it a little. Neither of us is sure."

Mom nodded. "Your father thinks she's wonderful."

"You're not sure you agree."

His mother shrugged. "I don't think anyone's good enough for you."

"Really?"

"You're such a smart boy, Damon."

He thought of pointing out that he was a man, but he knew her response would not be the one he hoped to hear. The only person who could give him that response was gone. He remembered Poppa lying in the hospital bed. He remembered the thin fingers and the sharp wit. He said, "You know, I don't think I ever thanked you."

"For what?" his mother asked.

1982

Damon sat at the kitchen table. He didn't want to stay at the kitchen table. He wanted to go outside and get high on the front steps and then go upstairs to the room he used to share with Leonard and sleep for an hour or two. He sat at the kitchen table and watched his mother smoke and drink scotch in the mid-afternoon.

"He's going to be fine," he told her.

"Probably. But still. You should go see him."

"I hate hospitals," Damon said.

"Everyone hates hospitals. But you go because the people who have to be there don't have a choice. It's a thing you do for another person."

"Did Leonard go to see him?"

"Truthfully, Damon? Poppa doesn't care if Leonard goes to see him. He likes Leonard well enough but you . . . he adores you."

"I adore him."

"So go see him."

"He's the only one who gets what I'm doing."

"I know, Honey. And it's good that you have that kind of connection. Even if it doesn't wind up being your life's work—"

"Don't do that, Mom."

"What? What am I doing?"

"This is what I do, Mom. This is what I'm good at."

"What do you know about what you do? You're eighteen years old."

"Do you know how many eighteen-year-olds are working as paid opening acts on the circuit right now?"

"How many?"

"Me."

"You have time, Damon. You could be anything, still. A doctor. A lawyer. A serious writer."

"You have no idea how seriously I take jokes."

His mother hissed like an epileptic snake.

"Why is that funny?"

"Because you sound just like my father when you talk like that."

"Not just like your father. If I sounded just like your father, I'd be spitting bits of white fish while I said it."

She hissed again.

"Go see him. He wants to see you. Go see him just in case."

1992

"You remember when Poppa was in the hospital and I didn't want to go see him?"

"You're thanking me for getting you to go see him?"

"What?" Damon said. "No. I'm thanking you for telling me that he adored me, that I meant more to him than Leonard, that I sounded just like him."

"I said that?"

"Yeah."

"I don't remember that."

He took a long drag on the joint and held his

breath. He turned the edge of the tip against the ash-tray to slow the burn and stop it from hotboxing. Re-leasing as little smoke as possible, he said, "Well, you did. And it meant a lot to me."

"You really like this girl," Mom said. She said it as a statement, not as a question.

Damon nodded, confirming her announcement.

"I want you to be happy, Damon. That's all your father and I want. We want you to be happy."

"That's not all you want, Mom. Come on. Seri-ously."

"What? What does that mean? Since when is that not what we want?"

Damon raised his eyebrows at her, wondering if she really didn't know.

1994

"You were thinking about it," his mother said. "Ever since you quit smoking pot, you think about telling me to quit smoking cigarettes."

"You have no idea what I think about."

They sat together in the kitchen haze. She took a long, slow sip of scotch. She said, "I don't know how I'm going to go through his things." She thought about the clothes in the closet. She thought about the tools in the garage. She imagined cardboard box-es. She couldn't imagine cardboard boxes strong enough to hold objects that had such weight at-tached to them, so many memories.

"You don't have to worry about that today, Mom. Take a little time."

She sighed. She turned the tip of her burning cigarette in the ashtray to clean away a bit of excess ash. As though it was a perfectly natural next thought she said, "You used to write such beautiful short stories. Do you remember those contests you won?"

"I'll tell you what, Mom," Damon said. "I won't tell you to quit smoking if you don't tell me to quit doing stand-up."

"I didn't say anything about that."

"You were working up to it," Damon said.

Mom shrugged. "Cynthia is all right at home alone?"

"She's fine. She's unpacking our stuff in the new place."

"Oh. That's right. You were moving this week."

"Yeah."

"Is there room in the new place for a nursery?"

"We have no interest in selling plants," Damon said.

"Ha ha," his mother said dryly. "Very funny. I get it."

"Do you?"

"I meant a baby's room, Damon. Have you discussed that? Neither of you is getting any younger, you know."

"So the answer would be, then, no. You don't get it."

"What do you mean?" his mother asked, blithely sipping her scotch.

Suddenly Damon found himself wishing he had never quit smoking grass. He tapped the metal splint on his finger against the kitchen table. "You wouldn't happen to have any Vicodin around here, would you?

Or Percocet?"

"Oh, Damon," his mother said. "Don't tell me you've gone and gotten yourself hooked on pills, now."

"No, Mom. I'm not hooked on pills," he said, which was entirely truthful. "But this thing is throbbing like hell and it makes it hard to think," which was not.

CHAPTER SIX

1994

Damon held the receiver to his ear with his injured hand. The other hand he used to draw small circles on the floor with the long, twisted cord. He stood very near to the phone as though that might prevent Leonard and Mom from hearing the conversation. He already had his suit pants and his tie on. His jacket, on a hanger, hung from the top of the door frame.

Damon tried to school his demeanor into an image of grief, which mainly presented simply as a tired slumping of the shoulders. He said, "Okay. This is very good. What time do I have to be there?"

He listened to Matthew's voice at the other end of the line. Matthew had a calm in his voice that Damon knew very well. It was a calm that spoke of controlled excitement, a refusal to give in to premature enthusiasm.

"Your set is at 9:45," he said. "But be there early if you possibly can."

"I can be there early," Damon said. "How long am I doing?"

"Six minutes. Not a second more."

"Six tight. Got it."

"I'm not kidding about this, Damon. You remember Comedy Blast?"

1987

L.A. Laughs opened its doors to the public at 8:00, but Damon was there at 7:30. His worn denim jacket and tight black jeans gave the impression that he had just wandered in from a Jackson Browne concert and had not been aware that he might be asked to perform this evening. He had gone to the back door and the kitchen staff let him in. He poured coffee for himself, so as not to bother a waitress or, more truthfully, so as not to feel obligated to tip anyone.

In the big room he sat at the back and looked at the empty stage. He felt very much at home at L.A. Laughs, almost the way he had felt at Mickey Tam's in New York before he moved. Twice a week he hosted the show here. This was not one of those nights.

He pulled a pen from his pocket and wrote notes on a napkin. He didn't write out whole jokes, just key words, the mnemonics, the titles of jokes that he intended to do. In some cases, he wrote a single word that represented a whole bit, three, five a run of seven jokes with tags and callbacks. It was his set list for the night and he had no real need of the napkin with the written words on it. He wouldn't look at it on stage like a bar band keeping track of the song order. He just wrote the list as a way of rehearsing, reviewing the order in his head. As he put the bits in order, he found new ways of getting from the end of one bit into the beginning of the next.

Damon always thought better, funnier, in the

last hours and minutes before he was to be on stage. Somehow the fact that he would soon be in front of an audience enabled him to better find the things he might say to that audience. Even in his imagination, the presence of the crowd was an essential element in his process.

He looked over the set list and knew that he had over-planned. He crossed off the word "legroom." He didn't need to do the joke tonight. It always got a good laugh, but he thought of it as generic, a line about airlines. Actually it was a joke about the way comics talk about airlines and more subtly it was a joke about the nature of generic comedy, a mean-spirited pot shot at comics who wrote jokes on over-used premises, working and reworking one another's ideas and pretending to present original thoughts.

Eight minutes. He was to do eight minutes. He had gotten used to doing twenty on this stage. He was comfortable on the road doing thirty as a feature act and sometimes he even ran the light now in road clubs, though he was careful only to do so when it was the last show of the evening. Running the light during the first show on a weekend screwed with the headliner's ability to do a full set or it put the whole show behind, making the second show start late and often setting up a pissed-off crowd.

There were so many elements to be balanced, jiggled, nudged into place to create the ideal circum-stance for a show to work right. Get the audience in on time, with drink orders taken before the start of the show. Music loud enough to get them working their diaphragms to talk in the pre-show period, but not so loud as to make them irritable or overly bois-terous. Room temperature below seventy-three, preferably considerably below. Waitresses and other club staff friendly, smiling, charming but never jokey, never quite bantering.

A lot of clubs on the road got few or none of the elements right. So many of them actually had only musicians' mic stands that Matthew had bought Damon a round-based, proper mic stand to take with him in his car when he did driving gigs. A mic stand with a tripod base just created obstacles on stage. Every toe tap against an extended aluminum leg thumped through the sound system like the *harrumph* of an impatient uncle. A boom stand that could be bent down to pick up an acoustic guitar was a disaster-in-waiting for a comic. An audience can't properly focus on a joke's set-up when it's watching the microphone slowly lean off to the side, away from the performer's mouth due to an improperly tightened wing nut. Damon had developed fast, easy saves to use on stage, seemingly improvisational, should such a thing happen, but it was always better to have a seamless show than a sloppy one held together with the duct-tape of corrective wit.

Duct tape was another thing Damon had taken to carrying with him when he could. A loose XLR cable connector could render a set unwatchable, humorless as the comic's voice boomed and then vanished randomly into conversational tones lost in the shush and murmur of a packed club. Damon had enough vocal power to ditch the mic entirely and project to the room when he had to, but he didn't have any proper theatrical vocal training. It was exhausting and changed the dynamic of his set dramatically. It was far more powerful to use the microphone and seem never to be pushing at all, not the breath, not the voice, not the jokes.

A few minutes before eight, Bobby the door guy let Matthew in to join him at the back of the room.

"I didn't know you were in here," Matthew said. "I was waiting out front with the civilians."

"I got here early."

"Yeah. You got a tight eight figured out?"

"I think so."

"Good." Matthew looked around from where he sat. Waitresses lit tea candles in red-tinted glass jars on each of the tables. The mic stood center stage in a proper, round-based stand. "Temperature's about right in here," he said.

"Yeah," Damon agreed. "Sam knows how to run a room. She's got it all goin'."

"Anything I need to worry about for you? Anything you need?"

"I'm good," Damon said. "Thanks."

"Okay," Matthew said. "I'm going to go get high in the car. Don't worry. I've got plenty for you for after the show."

Damon nodded.

"Listen. You do this right, keep it down to a tight eight, rock the room. This could be a game-changer. You know?"

Damon heard the controlled tension in Matthew's voice, the refusal to be excited, the care he was taking not to be a premature counter of chickens. "I've got it, Matthew. Go get high. I'm under control."

1984

"Who's that?" Poppa asked gruffly.

"This is Matthew, Poppa. He's going to manage me."

"He looks like a civilian."

"He is. But he's good. It's okay."

Poppa looked at Matthew with more than a touch of suspicion and opened the heavy door to allow both young men into the club. At ten thirty on a Saturday, the Friars' club was not yet open officially, but Poppa knew people. People liked him. He had told Damon it was important so Damon had come. He had said it was about his stand-up career, so Damon had brought Matthew. At twenty-one, Matthew seemed very adult to Damon. He seemed wise. Also, he had said he wanted to be Damon's manager and Damon liked the idea of having someone he could introduce as his manager.

"How many clients you got?" Poppa asked Matthew.

"Just Damon," Matthew said.

"Good," Poppa said. "You know it could be a long time before you make a living off him. Yeah? Comedy ain't a right-away-you-make-a-million-dollars kind of job."

"Yeah," Matthew said. He chewed as though there was something in his mouth.

Damon knew that he was self-conscious about his upbringing, that he didn't like people to know about his parents, his trust fund, his utter lack of financial concerns. Damon said, "Don't worry, Poppa. He knows what we're about here."

Poppa nodded. He made the decision to let it go.

Damon had taken an early train in from New Jersey and Matthew had met him at Penn Station. Damon had guesses as to what Poppa wanted, but none of those guesses was right. He was not going to the Friars' Club to be introduced to important people in the comedy industry or to be privately initiated into the club. Poppa did not want to help him get booked as an opener for Stevie Kahn or Howie "the Madman" Chuckner. What Poppa wanted was far more practical. In the long run, it was far more useful.

Poppa led Matthew and Damon through the empty bar and Damon saw that he shuffled a bit now, more than he had realized. Poppa had really become an old man. His shoes looked a little loose on his feet. His jacket had become worn at the cuffs and Damon wondered if his grandfather had decided he was so close to death that it no longer mattered whether he replaced his clothing.

The show room at the Friars' Club smelled of tradition and flop sweat, laughter and booze. It also smelled of carpet powder and fried food. To Damon, the complex compound of odors seemed very romantic. Elegant. Nostalgic, in a way that reached beyond the fringe of his own memory into memories that lived in black-and-white movies. "Go up on the stage while I talk to you," Poppa said. Then, to Matthew, "You sit out here with me."

Matthew and Poppa sat down at a table halfway to the back of the room as Damon walked up the worn flower-patterned carpet to the stage. He climbed up the little set of black-painted steps and stood behind the microphone. He wondered if Poppa was going to make him do his act. He didn't want that. It felt wrong to perform for two people he knew on a weekend day. It felt wrong to perform with the house lights up and the stage lights down. He also felt a wave of nervousness. Poppa had never seen him perform before. He'd heard some of the jokes. He'd heard a cassette tape recording once. But those weren't the same thing at all. Neither was standing in an empty room, doing a set to two people he knew. Surely Poppa would understand such a thing.

"Take the thing out," Poppa said.

"What?" Damon asked.

"The thing. The microphone. Out of the thing."

"The stand?"

"Yeah."

Damon took the mic from the stand.

"Put it back," Poppa said.

"What are we doing?" Damon asked, tapping on the mic head to see if it was even turned on.

"Practicing. Put the thing back in the thing."

Damon guided the cord through the gap in the mic cradle and replaced the device in the stand.

"Good. Do that a hundred more times while I talk at you."

Damon did as he was told. He wanted to hear what his grandfather had to say. He always wanted to hear what his grandfather had to say and this trip to the Friars' Club had felt more like a command than a request. There was an urgency in all of it for Poppa and it seemed to be contagious.

"Your first paid jobs are going to be as an opener. An emcee. Here are the rules for a good emcee. You ready?" He did not wait for a response. "You greet the audience. You thank them for coming. You introduce yourself. All of that is earnest and honest. You are the host. Do your act. Don't think you're wasting it just 'cause you're doing it to a crowd that's not warmed up yet. Don't think you have to do crowd work to make them comfortable. What makes them comfortable is the knowledge that they are in the hands of a professional. That means making them laugh. Do your act. Ten minutes. Fifteen. Whatever the club owner or the booker tells you. Not a minute more."

Damon took the mic out of the stand. He put the mic back into the stand.

"You get each performer's intro information before you go on stage and you commit it to memory. Whatever they want. Credits, where he's from. Whatever. You learn it so you don't have to read it. Always give the impression that you know the person and are fully aware of his credits and history. You're always impressed with the person, excited to bring them to the stage, happy to be working with them. Doesn't matter if it's a dog shit, pathetic hack of a prop act. You are the host to both the audience and the performers. You are introducing the former to the latter by introducing the latter to the former."

The sentence surprised Damon. It didn't sound like his grandfather, somehow. It sounded wrong. He studied his grandfather, back there in the middle of the room and put the mic back into the stand by feel.

"Good!" Poppa said. "How many is that?"

"Rules?"

"No, shmuck. How many times with the thing in the thing."

"Oh! I forgot to count. Twenty, maybe. Twenty-five?"

"Good. Do ten more and then we're going on to something else. Now. When you do the intro, it's credits first if there are any. Then personal stuff. Then the very last thing is the person's name. You say, 'This next guy, is Jacob Dorfman. He's from Rhode Island and he's been on TV,' you've fucked up the first five minutes of the poor guy's show. How do you do that intro?"

"Um . . . that'd be . . . 'this next guy has been on TV, he's a very funny man from Rhode Island. Jacob Dorfman.'"

"Not bad. Now do it like you're introducing two people at a party. One of 'em's named Ladies and Gentlemen. Go."

"Okay. Uh . . . Hey! I want to introduce you to this guy. He's been on Live from the Chucklehut on WMOX, Public Television out of Trenton and he's just gotten in from Rhode Island. Ladies and gentlemen, I'd like you to meet Jacob Dorfman."

"Not too bad. It sounds a little *too* much like what I said, but you get the idea. Yeah?"

"Yeah. Yeah, I do."

"You gotta make everyone comfortable with everyone else and you gotta lead up to the name. It's how they're trained. The audience, I mean. Then they know exactly when to clap and the whole rhythm of the thing works right. If you don't cue the audience right, they can't play their part right. Okay. Next thing. You ready?"

Damon was very ready for the next thing. Everything his grandfather had said seemed comfortingly familiar yet entirely new. It was nothing he had ever thought about, but a lot of it was stuff he had already started doing when he had to do an introduction. He was surprised he hadn't ever thought about the order of the introduction. He had spent so much time, even before he'd started performing, thinking about the way a joke needed to be ordered, how the set-up led to the punch line, how the fewer words it took to get there the better the laugh was.

"Yes," he said. "Next thing."

"Good. Take the thing out of the thing."

"Didn't we do that already?"

"Shut up."

Damon took the microphone from the stand.

"Good. Hold it like you're gonna talk into it."

Damon did.

"Now, run your free hand down the cord until your whatsitcalled is straight."

"My gay cousin Mikey?"

"That's funny. No."

"Good. 'Cause I don't know how I could do that by running my hand down the cord."

"Your elbow. Until your elbow is straight."

"Ah." Damon did that.

"Give the cord a little tug to pull extra slack up onto the stage and then pull the part you're holding up to make a loop and hold that against the mic, so the cord isn't just hanging straight down from it."

"Like this?" Damon did the thing that had been described and immediately recognized the gesture as something he'd seen on TV and in clubs. Something that felt like Vegas to him. Something that felt like Sammy Davis Junior.

"Yeah. Now there's no chance you're gonna accidentally unplug your own mic. You gotta know these things. Actors learn how to hit the back row without blowing their voices out. How to find the key light. Whatever. Dancers learn how to stretch. Doctors learn how to hold a scalpel. There's no BFA in comedy. This is the technical stuff you gotta learn and nobody's gonna teach you."

"Okay. So, loop the cord."

"Yeah. Loop the cord. Then put the mic away. Then pull it out and loop the cord again. I got more to say while you keep doing that."

Damon practiced his cord-looping technique while Poppa talked. He found that he was almost unaware of the process now when he pulled the mic free and put it back.

"I'm about halfway to the back of the house. Show lights were up, you couldn't see me. Doesn't matter. Figure out what it feels like when this is what you're lookin' at. How you hold your head. Your shoulders. Also, when you look at the back of the room. Now. While you can see it. When the show lights are going and the house lights are down, you'll wanna look at the people in the front, and you can do that sometimes too. But you gotta look at the back some. The people in front already feel connected to you. They can see the sweat on your lip, the spit when you make a C-H word. The people in the back and the middle. They're the ones you gotta look at. Make 'em feel like you're talkin' right to them even though they're just gray blobs in the dark sea."

Damon put the mic back into the stand. He took it out again.

"You're doing good with the mic there, kid. Shit. There's so much."

"So much what?"

"So much shit nobody ever told me," Poppa said. "So much shit I never really thought about before that I gotta tell you now."

"This is good, Poppa," Damon said. "What you just told me. You can tell me more another time."

"You should put in your intro, 'Been on stage at the Friars' Club.'"

Damon chuckled.

"That's not a joke. That's a good credit, I just gave you."

"Okay, Poppa."

"Now, loosen the thing on the thing so you can make it go up and down."

"The mic stand?"

"What'd I just say?"

"The tension lock?"

"The thing that holds it there. You gotta be able to make it taller or shorter without fighting with it. Practice. I got more to say."

At some point Matthew had pulled out a small notebook and he was writing frantically in it, taking notes, Damon guessed.

1987

Damon stood beside Matthew, smelling the pot smoke captured in his young manager's wool jacket. Matthew seemed very relaxed now, very comfortable.

Toby, the emcee went back up on stage. "Let him hear it, ladies and gentlemen. Show him the love. Hugh Lombart!" The audience applauded politely. "Okay," the emcee said. "Our next act, this guy – um

–" he pulled a slip of paper from his pocket. "Hang on. He wrote down some things . . . Damon Blazer's been on stage at clubs and colleges all over the country. He's a house emcee some nights right here at L.A. Laughs and he's pretty funny. So let's give it up for him."

There was a little bit of scattered applause as Damon sighed and began moving toward the stage. The emcee scolded the audience for not clapping enough. "Come on, people! Let him hear it! Bring him up here right!" The applause built just a bit as Damon came on stage.

He offered a hand to shake Toby's and whispered, "Thanks. Nice job," to the emcee. It was a lie, but it was what he had been taught to do. "Always whisper something friendly and nice to the emcee when you get brought up," his grandfather had told him. "Make him feel good about himself. Audience thinks you're friends, you know each other, you share secrets about 'em and hang out in the back together. Hookers. Blow. Whatever. Makes 'em think you're all in the same club together and they're being allowed in with you."

Damon stepped up behind the microphone.

He was going to have to fix the damage done by the bad intro. He hated to waste some of his brief showcase on that sort of a task. He had a thought and went with it.

"Hi, folks," he said. "Before I get started . . ." He hoped by saying that he would get the house manager to delay the start on the clock by a joke or two. ". . . I gotta tell you how nice it is to be here with all of you. I flew back in from New York just this morning. I had an exhausting flight. I flew Continental. They're running that new promotional package; you bring a spare part, you fly free . . . ?" He always made that sound like a question, as though he expected the audience to know about the available deal. Then he could let them laugh as though he was just making sure they were up to speed. "I was thinking about all the comics I hear complaining about flying. 'Oooh, there's not enough leg room.' Really? 'Cause I think there's about thirty-thousand feet of leg room. How much more of it do you want access to?" The audience laughed, a good laugh, a real laugh. They were with him. He'd turned them back into a crowd faster than he'd thought. He couldn't just ditch the bit now and shift to something else entirely. He went on. "The food? Why complain? They're getting you across a continent in a few hours and you're ragging on them for a lack of catering skills? Seat cushions that can turn into floatation devices, that's nothing! They've glued wings on a bus and turned it into an anti-gravity machine." On the road he would have said, "a fucking bus," and maybe "a fucking anti-gravity machine." But not tonight. Not in front of the Comedy Blast people. Not when he had the audience in the palm of his hand and he was just about to get to his eight minutes of showcase material.

1994

"Check in with Cynthia," he said. "Make sure she's okay, wouldja? And . . . I'll call you after the thing tonight. I'll let you know how it goes." He hung up the phone and waited for it. It came almost immediately.

"Are you fucking kidding me?" Leonard asked. In his suit slacks but still shirtless, he slurped cereal out of a bowl with a soup spoon. "You got a thing tonight?"

"I am not kidding you, Leonard. When I kid you, there'll be humor content." Then, after half a beat, "Although you might not recognize it."

"In the city?" his mother asked.

"Yeah. I can get the six o'clock train. I'll have plenty of time."

"You're unbelievable," Leonard said. "You're gonna just take off from Dad's funeral and run to the train station to go do jokes for strangers. That's your idea of . . . you know . . . respect?"

"Matthew got me a showcase for Letterman, Len. It's kind of a big deal."

"Oh!" his mother said. "I watch that show sometimes. I watch it in bed with . . . I used to watch it in bed with your father." The series of twitches and spasms that bent her face as she reviewed that sentence made Damon worry about her for a moment, but only for a moment. Then she said, "Leonard, finish getting dressed. We don't want to be late for this."

"Not if Damon's gonna have to leave early."

"He won't, Dear," Mom said. "We're not going to do the whole thing again, like we did with Poppa."

At that Damon chuckled, because he remembered what she meant by "the whole thing," and for all that had gone on the day that his grandfather was buried, that had been the part that he found the most hilarious.

CHAPTER SEVEN

1994

Damon stepped into the IMPROV on 45th Street and a wave of relief and relaxation swept through him. The transition from the sounds and smells of Manhattan to the club's interior was a familiar shift, nostalgic. The place hadn't changed. The texture of the lighting made it an Edward Hopper painting. The sound of drinks being poured, of pens scratching at notebooks, of quiet conversation in the bar outside the showroom, were all exactly as they had been the first time he walked through that door as a teenager.

Despite the time he had spent away from the place, the new faces and the changes in the old, he could read the dynamics. He could see the nervousness on the faces of those who were new to the game. He knew the resentments and hostilities of those who had been around for too long without advancement. He knew the arrogance of those who were on the rise and believed themselves to be on a clear trajectory toward stardom. He took it all in and after two days with his family in the house of his childhood, this was like coming home.

1984

Damon walked into the IMPROV at 7:45. The show would start at 8:00. Damon was scheduled to take the stage around 12:30am. He moved to the bar and ordered a cup of coffee.

Stu, the bartender poured him a cup and put half-and-half in a tiny metal pitcher next to it on the bar. Damon added cream to the cup and stirred it in slowly.

The coffee was served in a brown plastic cup that was designed to look like glazed ceramic. It gave it a classy look, but he had learned long ago that once he lifted the cup from the bar, the illusion would be shattered. The mug was too light, even full. It felt cheap. It always felt a little bit like he'd been cheated when he picked it up, deceived in a tiny but hurtful way. He wanted to write jokes about that, but he couldn't quite find a way in to it. He didn't want to make fun of the club for its coffee cups. He'd learned not to make fun of the club's offerings after his second suspension.

He sat at the bar and stalled for a moment, letting himself enjoy the deception now before picking up the cup and sipping from it. He realized that almost nobody drank coffee at the club other than him and Stu. When he brought coffee on stage with him, the audience never knew that the cup was too light, that it was not exactly as it appeared. He wondered if that might be the way to talk about it. No. Nothing funny there that he could see.

He put a finger on the corner of a cocktail napkin and spun the paper square on the varnished surface of the bar.

"You always get here early," Stu said.

"Yeah," Damon said.

Stu went on with what he was doing. "Even when you've got a late spot, you get here early."

"Yeah."

Stu washed a glass in the bar sink and put it away, getting ready for the other comics to start showing up, the few, scattered audience members who would be there at the start of a weeknight show.

"You get here before the show starts when you got the last spot of the night."

"Yeah."

"And you stay 'til the end if you got the first spot of the night."

"Yeah."

"Why is that?"

"I like to watch the other acts. I'm still sort of trying to figure out what the hell I'm doing."

"No shit?" Stu said.

That surprised him. "Yeah. What do you mean?"

"You been in here for—what?—a year or so? How long have you been doing this?"

"Yeah. I got in last year. I started open miking in '82."

Stu nodded then and didn't say anything. Damon had had the distinct impression that Stu was going somewhere with the conversation, but now it had fallen apart.

"My parents are coming in to see me tonight," he offered.

"Nice," Stu said.

"Maybe," Damon said.

1984

Damon stood on the stage at the Friars' Club coiling and holding the mic cord, returning the mic to the stand, taking it out again, coiling and holding the mic cord.

"I invited my parents to come to the IMPROV."

"Don't expect 'em to laugh like normal   people," Poppa said from halfway back in the empty house.

"What do you mean?"

"Your parents are civilians, Damon. It's important that you know that. They're smart, and your Dad is funny sometimes. But they're civilians. Both of them. Your Mom . . . she didn't have to be. But she is. And they're worse. They're academic civilians. You ever go to a movie with 'em?"

"Of course."

"You ride home; they don't like the movie or dislike the movie. They approve or disapprove."

Damon laughed comfortably. "I might have to find a way to use that."

"On stage it'll need–"

"Yeah."

"Okay."

"So, you think they won't be able to watch me without judging the act?"

"They won't be able to watch you without judging everything. Your act, the venue, the lighting, the French fries. That's how they are. But that's not really what I'm talking about."

"What are you talking about, then?"

"I'm saying, don't expect them to laugh like normal people. Don't let it throw you if you hear them in the crowd. It'll stand out. You'll know the sound of them."

"How do they laugh?"

"Your father, he snorts. And it's never just a snort that says, 'that's funny.' It's always a snort that says five or eight different things and one of them is always, 'I'm smarter than you.'"

"What about Mom?"

"My daughter has the worst laugh in the world when you're performing. She thinks, I don't know, she thinks it's a knowing laugh. Or it makes her seem like . . . not a civilian. But you can hear it no matter how big the crowd is. She hisses. Like a snake sending you morse code in the middle of a show. 'Sss. Sss. Sss.' It's like she's trying to stop the air from leaking out of her emotional life."

Damon laughed again. He knew the laugh his grandfather was describing. He knew it the way he knew the sound of the water running in the kitchen sink, the way he knew the tapping of the pine tree's branches against his bedroom window. It was a sound he had known so well, for so long, that he barely heard it anymore. But he knew the moment Poppa said it that it was a sound that could reach him over all other sounds in a crowded, happy room.

1984

Stu nodded past Damon's shoulder and said, "That them?"

Damon said, "What?" and spun around.

His parents had arrived. They were the first people to arrive. It was twelve minutes to eight and his parents had arrived for his twelve-thirty performance.

"Hey!" he said, hoping they had just stopped by to check the place out before going elsewhere for dinner. "You're early."

"Yeah," his father said. "With the cover charge and the drink minimums and everything, we figured we'd get our money's worth. See the whole show."

Stu snickered softly, a friendly, quiet sort of snicker that was unlikely to be heard by anyone but Damon, who was still very close to the bar.

"There's nobody here," Damon's mother said.

"It's a weeknight, Mom. The show generally starts a little slow."

"Oh!" she said. "All right. Well, we'll just get started on that drink minimum while we wait for things to get underway."

They moved together toward the show room. Dad offered Damon a grin and a supportive wink as he walked with her, a hand gentle against her lower back as they moved into the dimmer darkness of the room beyond the showroom door. Damon sighed.

He let them get inside, left enough time for them to get settled and then followed them in, carrying his

underweighted coffee cup with him. He took his usu-
al position at the back booth just inside the door.
This was his spot, his vantage point. It was from here
that he watched the other comics, the ones who got
the prime-time spots, the ones who had been doing it
for years and had worked the road, the cruises, Vegas. From back there in the darkness he watched
Carol Pensky and Ronny Dahl and Jerry B. Davis doing their acts to full rooms at nine thirty, at ten
o'clock. He learned how much of the off-the-cuff ad-
libbing was made up of lines they did in every show,
creating the perfect illusion of spontaneity every
time. From back here he could see the glint when a
brand new joke got its first laugh, the flicker of effort
when a true ad-lib worked well and needed to be
memorized fast, in the duration of an in-breath, for
future use.

Tonight though, in these moments before the
house lights dimmed and the emcee opened the
show, Damon watched his parents sitting together in
the large, empty space. He watched them ordering
drinks from the waitress as they looked over the dinner menu. He imagined their response to the greasy
food that would come to them, their judgment of the
drinks, their size, their strength, their cost. He imagined their odd, audible laughter in the club during
the first acts when they were the only ones there or
among the few. He imagined their odd, audible
laughter later on during the prime-time acts. He imagined their odd, audible laughter during his 12:30
set when the club was almost empty once more.

He began to wish that he had not invited them at
all.

A party of three came in and took a front table   a

minute before the emcee took the stage, so it wasn't just his parents when the show started. Syd Tyler did a few minutes of "Where you from? Whattaya do for a living?" with the small house as more audience trickled in.

From the back of the room, Damon found he could not watch the performance, could not watch the first comic as he took the stage for his set, could not properly listen to the jokes, study the technique, follow the act. All he could do was watch the backs of his parents' heads. He read their tensions. He knew exactly what was being whispered each time Dad leaned in close to Mom for a moment.

By nine o'clock they had finished their comedy club dinner long ago and he had seen them signal the waitress three times to ask for more drinks. Only twice had he heard his mother's hissing laugh cut through the sound of the room and his father had not snorted knowingly at all. He had grunted unhappily a few times during the act of Paulie Dubai, a black man who did a great deal of self-hating racist material, occasionally punctuated with excuses. "I can say this, 'cause I'm black. Y'all can't say it, or you'll get beat up outside the club. But I can say it, 'cause I'm a brother. You understand?" Most of the crowd ate it up. Most of most crowds did.

At nine-twenty, Tom Deleo came off stage and Damon's father got up and walked toward the back of the room. Damon assumed he was going to the restroom until his father signaled him to come out to the bar. Damon followed him out of the show room. They stood together in the quiet bar. His father leaned close as though he was still whispering in the audience, but he spoke a little louder than necessary because of all the drinks.

"Listen," he said, "Your mother's getting tired and some of these comics are just . . . awful."

"Uh-huh," Damon said.

"Do you think you could talk to them about, you know, putting you up sooner?"

"I really can't, Dad. These are the prime-time spots. I can't just ask for a prime-time spot at this point 'cause Mom is tired. I go up early, or I go up late. I told you I wouldn't be up 'til after twelve."

"Yeah. I know."

"I told you you didn't have to get here 'til eleven, eleven-thirty."

"We just didn't realize it was going to be so . . ." Dad trailed off. Then he said, "So, there's no way you can get up any earlier, then?"

"No. Really. Sorry."

"Okay. I'll—okay. That's fine. Okay." He turned and moved back into the showroom, his hand touching the doorway as he passed through it into the darkness.

Damon stayed at the bar. He signaled Stu for another cup of coffee and rested the side of his face on his hand.

"Sounds like they picked a good night to come see you," Stu said.

"What?"

"Good crowd. Sounds loud in there."

"Yeah. Yeah. I guess."

It was true. The room had filled nicely over the course of the evening. Everyone seemed to be getting a pretty good response. Damon hadn't really noticed that much at all. He tried to focus on that now. He sat at the bar and listened to the rising waves of laughter filtering out. He counted seconds between the laughs like a child gauging the distance of lightning. Things were going well. Fifteen seconds between. Twelve. Nice. Someone had the rhythm in there.

At ten forty-five, Damon's parents emerged from the showroom. They both staggered just a bit, the controlled stagger of the functional drunk. Dad waved him over from the bar and he joined them at the showroom door then moved with them further away into the bar, so they could talk.

"I'm sorry, Buddy," his father said. "We can't stay through anymore of this."

"We didn't realize it was going to be such a long night," his mother said.

"You're leaving. That's what you're telling me, isn't it?"

"Don't do that," Mom said. "Don't turn this into something we're doing to you."

"I told you not to come until—"

"You know what, Honey? You did. That's true. But you certainly didn't tell us it was going to be so racist and sexist and . . . vulgar." Mom made a little shivering gesture as though the whole experience had been so horrific she could only hope, some day, to shake off the memory.

Dad winced at Damon, an empathetic gesture of support as though he understood how hurtful his wife's words and actions might be. Then he reached out to shake Damon's hand, to wrap him in a hug and slurred into his ear, "We're going home, Buddy. You can come with us." Then, as if he was giving Damon permission that he imagined the young man desperately craved he said, "You don't have to do this if you don't want to. You could be a great writer."

Then it was Damon's turn to wince.

1994

Stu squeezed between people at the crowded bar and approached Damon. He grinned, extending a hand.

"Damon! Man, great to have you back, kid."

"Looks like things are goin' good here. Huh?"

"Unbelievable," Stu said. "It can't last forever but the last couple of years . . . packed every night. Weekends we're breaking it into two shows now. It's the TV stuff. *Comic Strip Live* started it. And the *A&E* thing. Everyone's coming out to the clubs."

"Yeah," Damon said. "My manager tells me if I land this Letterman thing . . ."

"Oh, hell, yeah. You'll be headlining clubs forty weeks outta the year, Baby. Listen, your people are already inside. I got Zucco on stage right now and he's killing. Is that alright for you or do you want someone else between him and you?"

"That's fine, man. Thanks. Put me up next."

"You got it, Baby. Listen, I'm running the room now all week. You meet the new bartender yet?"

"Not yet."

"Still coffee?"

"Yeah. Thanks."

"Lemme get that for you."

And he pushed back in through the crowd.

Damon pulled the splint off his finger and set it on the little shelf behind the host's stand. He worked his hand a bit to make sure it would function if he needed to adjust the microphone or the stand. The last thing he needed tonight was to look clumsy or amateurish.

CHAPTER EIGHT

1994

Damon stood at the back of the room. He listened to the introduction. It was almost dead right. The emcee got one of his credits wrong, but nobody would ever know that. The order was right, at least. His name was the last thing the young man said and the audience applauded loudly on cue. He walked up the aisle casually, coffee cup in hand, to take the stage. He shook the hand of the emcee as they passed one another on the stage. He leaned in smiling and whispered, "Nicely done. Thanks."

The emcee whispered something back, but Damon didn't hear what it was. He didn't care. He moved the stool to where he wanted it, beside him as a place to put his coffee. He glanced up at the lights to make sure he was in the best place to catch the key. He adjusted the microphone just a bit, angling it slightly more toward his mouth. He sighed. Someone in the audience chuckled.

Damon turned sharply toward the sound, startled, perhaps a little offended. More people laughed and his head snapped again looking into the darkness as though he suspected something was going on of which he was unaware. Slowly, he set down his coffee cup on the stool, still eyeing the crowd suspiciously. It seemed he feared that if he looked away they would begin talking about him behind his back. Or worse, laughing again.

He noticed someone at the front table with a cup of coffee. He did something he hadn't planned on doing. Despite a requirement to do a tight six to showcase for Letterman, he did something he hadn't planned on doing.

1987

Damon came off the stage at L.A. Laughs and heard the roaring applause of the happy crowd. He knew he had owned the room. There was no question in his mind. He had run a minute or two long but that shouldn't matter much. He had been funny as hell. He had fixed the problem created by the crap emcee, he had won them over, warmed them up for himself and then he had rocked the room for the eight minutes he had been asked to do. Surely anybody who had an eye for comedy would have seen that, would have understood the nature of his decision.

He moved down the dark aisle toward the exit, listening to the applause continue. He knew the emcee had to be back on stage by now, but still they clapped for him.

Damon stepped outside into the cool night air in time to hear a young man in a tie say to Matthew, "I'm not saying it wasn't a great set. Your guy's very funny. But if he's gonna be on TV, he has to learn how to stick to his time."

1982

"Fuck that," Poppa said. "You have plenty of time. Every time you take the stage, you wait before you talk. Every time. Look around. Take it all in. Let 'em start to worry you don't know what you're doing. Make sure that if anybody in the room is nervous it's the audience, not you. You get me? There's never a rush."

"Really?"

"I ever give you bad advice?"

Poppa picked up a shiny steel medical device from the bedside table. He turned a little crank that made it open and close.

"Don't play with that, Poppa. It's not a toy."

"You should tell the nurse. You should see the game she likes to play with this thing."

"That's funny."

"Thank you. I tried to do it for your mother. She kept saying, 'Put that down. Put that down.' The only joke I could do was, 'Fine. It's an ugly probe and it repeated the third grade four times.'"

"How'd it go over?"

"She hissed."

Damon had trouble believing that his mother had actually hissed at the little joke. He assumed that his grandfather was exaggerating for comedic effect so he chuckled.

"Listen, Damon. I'm serious about this time thing. You can wait. Take in what's going on as best you can. Sometimes you'll find out the jokes you were gonna do aren't gonna work for some reason. Sometimes you'll see something you need to talk about or else it'll be all anyone's thinking about. Quadriplegic in the front row. Guy in a Carmen Miranda fruit hat. Whatever. You know?"

"Sort of."

"You can't always just go on stage with a plan and stick with it. That's not the way the thing works. Sometimes you plan to say, 'You should see the games we play with this thing,' and you have to say, 'It's ugly and stupid,' instead. You know?"

"That's better."

"What?"

"'The games we play with this thing.' That's better than, 'The games she likes to play with this thing.'"

Poppa nodded. He turned his lips down at the corners. "Yeah," he said. "I think you're right."

1987

Damon turned to the pair and approached them. He knew it was the wrong thing to do even as he did it, but he did it anyway. He approached them, already working up a head of anger.

"Are you kidding me, Man?" he asked. "Are you fucking kidding me?"

The young man was startled. He took half a step back, afraid he might actually be coming under physical attack. "Hi, Damon. You were very funny tonight," the young man said. "I'm Kirk Taymenshock from—"

"I know who you are," Damon said. "Do you know what I just did? Did you hear the crappy intro? I turned a confused crowd back into an audience for myself. I cooked. I killed. I owned that room."

"You did, Man. Nobody's saying otherwise. But the thing is—"

"Oh, fuck this. Seriously. Fuck this."

Damon walked back into the club, leaving Matthew to see if he could clean up the mess.

1994

"You're having the coffee," Damon said to the guy in the front row. He lifted his own cup from the stool in a toasting gesture of camaraderie and the man raised his cup back at him. "The cups are weird, aren't they?"

The audience chuckled a bit nervously, having no idea what to make of this observation, but Damon's fellow coffee drinker blurted out, "Yeah! They are!" and then the room laughed just because the response was so authentic, so heartfelt.

Damon brought them in with an explanation. "They're too light. They look like regular cups, but they're made of plastic. So there's this second when you first go to take a sip that you think, 'Man! I am suddenly very, very strong.'" The audience laughed. "Grrrr. Hulk drink coffee!" They laughed. "Every time I get coffee here it happens. I order the coffee and it comes and I think, 'Hey! That's a good looking cup of coffee. That's very. . . classy.' And then I pick it up and I think, 'Hey! They lied to me! That's not classy at all. That's disappointing.'" The audience laughed, understanding, recognizing, knowing now what sort of cups these were, what the hell Damon was talking about. "Then I hate myself for a moment for being so vulnerable, so pathetic that I can experience a wave of disappointment over the weight of a coffee cup." They laughed a little, light sympathetic laugh. "But it is. It's disappointing." He sipped the coffee. "Not as disappointing as the coffee *itself.*" The room filled with laughter. Damon spoke sheepishly into the microphone, "That's the kind of stuff that used to get me suspended from the club every couple of months." He took another sip from the cup and as he went to set it down he muttered, off-handedly, "Mmmm. Hulk sip." And the audience laughed hard and clapped for him.

CHAPTER NINE

1994

Damon leaned his head against the cool Plexiglas window of the airplane and watched the east- coast color palate turn into a distant,   blurred image. He allowed himself to whipsaw internally between controlled elation and crushing skepticism. It was possible that he had not fully understood what Matt had said on the phone, or that he had over- valued it. It was possible that Matt had not fully understood what Linda DuMont had said or had over-valued it.

This was one of the effects, he knew, of the time spent in Los Angeles. He had slowly become less and less able to distinguish reality when it came to promises made, offers proffered verbally. In L.A., people said things off-handedly without regard for the impact it might have on the listener. They said, "Let's work together soon," or, "You might be just the guy for this script I'm producing," or, "I want you on my show," and frequently meant only that they had enjoyed seeing you perform, or that they had enjoyed having lunch with you, or that they liked your shirt.

Damon had wrapped up tightly when he saw the light from the back of the club. He knew he had done very well on stage. He knew the laughs had come steadily, that he'd had a good rhythm, a loose, improvisational feel even as he moved through the carefully structured set. He had chosen only short bits that he knew were packed with laughs, guaranteed material that included no vulgarity, no particular risk or controversy. The opening lines about the coffee cup had been new to the stage, but not entirely new to him. That piece had been formulating in his brain for quite some time and he was fairly certain of it when he started speaking, though he was afraid as he did that he was self-sabotaging, ruining his chances of making good with the showcase.

Once that bit had worked so well, though, he had known his whole set was going to be sharp. Also, he had written one absolutely new line in that moment, one that made the coffee cup piece something he might be able to use over and over again. "Hulk sip." To Damon's mind, that was a perfect joke. Two syllables, able to be thrown away and such a great juxtaposition of words. "Hulk sip." He half wondered if he hadn't landed Letterman the moment those two words left his lips.

He hadn't landed Letterman. It was important to remember that. Not yet. There was no date yet, no plane ticket back to New York yet, no actual offer.

He had written one great line on stage. That was the thing to hold on to. Regardless of what happened with Letterman, he had written a great new line on stage and had tried out a new bit and done a good set. That was the important stuff. One way or the other, the evening was a success. Hang on to that. Let the rest of it go. That was the way to avoid disappointment.

1984

"Now let's talk about the stand," Poppa said.

"What do we need to talk about?"

"First of all, what you got there is the right kind of stand. You always want that kind of stand. Tripod stands trip you up. Bendy stands—"

"Boom stands?" Matthew offered.

"Whatever, they can ruin a show. You always want a straight, round-based stand."

"Okay," Damon said.

"Put the mic back in and tilt the stand on the edge of the base. Feel it out. Find out how far it can go before it tips over."

Damon did as he was told.

"Now put your foot on the edge of the base so's you can control it. Push it away . . . then make it go back by stepping on the base. When's your next spot at the Improv?"

Damon glanced at Matthew. Matthew looked down intently at his notes.

"What?" Poppa said. "What was that? What's going on?"

"I got suspended at the Improv, Poppa. Three weeks. No spots."

"Suspended? What the hell is that? Is this a comedy club or a middle school?

"I pissed off the owner."

1984

Damon glanced down at the front table as the man who sat there poured wine into his date's glass. The glugging sound drew his attention and he felt certain that it had been loud enough to distract everyone in the club.

His mind raced. He knew he'd been in the middle of something. A set-up. But now that moment was gone, to go back to it after stopping abruptly would give up any sense of spontaneity he had created thus far. The moment was going on too long. He had no jokes about the glugging sound. He had no way of going back to what he had been saying. He forced himself to breathe against the rising panic. He slowed down, trying to take in the moment, to find something to say that would bring the audience into his thought process.

The man in the front row noticed him staring at the bottle. He held it up as though he was offering Damon some. Damon reached down and took the bottle from him. He read the label. The scattered audience chuckled, watching the action, as uncertain as to where it was leading as Damon was himself. Damon raised his eyebrows as though something had startled him about the bottle. The crowd chuckled again.

"This is the good stuff," he said. Then, "Ed's Wine." The audience laughed. "See ball-point pen offer on back." The house wasn't anywhere near full, but for just a moment, it seemed to be overflowing with laughter and scattered clapping.

1984

Poppa laughed, slapping the table. "Idiots! That's a good joke."

"Yeah. But apparently it was the house wine and they didn't like me saying that about it."

"Fuck that, Damon. What do they know? You're not there to tell people how good their wine is. You're there to be funny as hell and that joke is funny as hell. You can use that joke . . . that's the kind of joke you can use over and over again. Sometimes it's the wine at the front table, sure. Sometimes it's–I don't know–'I like the cheap stuff. Ed's Wine. See ball-point pen offer on back.' Or a girlfriend. 'No taste in wine. Oooh. Ed's Wine. See ball-point pen offer . . .' That's a great joke, kid. Good work."

"Thanks." Damon tipped the stand. He righted it with his foot.

"You write a joke like that on stage, you write a joke like that on the spot while you're working, that night is a big success. I don't care what else is going on in the room. Glasses are falling on the floor. People are fighting. This thing where they suspend you. I don't care. You write a joke like that, kid, that's a good night."

1974

Damon turned a bit of toasted waffle on the plate with his fork. It had been three minutes since he'd been scolded for doing George Carlin's joke, and three minutes since he had been presented with the idea of joke-writing. He kept his focus on the chunk of food as it rotated in a pool of syrup. He said, fairly quietly, "Okay. What about this?"

Dad did not look up from his puzzle as he said, "What?"

Poppa focused fully on him though. Damon knew, though he didn't know exactly how he knew, that he had to stay fully focused on his plate or he wouldn't be able to get through the words, wouldn't be able to keep them in the right order. Even if he could, somehow, it was important that he be looking down, offering the whole thing almost as a tentative question.

"One iguana says to another iguana, 'Hello,' and the other iguana says, 'Hello,' and the first iguana says, 'Hey! Is there a gecko in here?'"

His mother said, "Ssss ssss ssss ssss ssss."

His father snorted a snort that said, "You got me," and also, "I should have seen that coming," and also, "Where the hell did that come from?"

Poppa, though. Poppa rose from his seat laughing a real, proper laugh. Damon's grandfather stood up, Alvie Grunman, the performer, the man who knew everything there was to know about comedy. Elevated by the joy of the sound coming from his own chest, he stood and lifted Damon out of his chair so abruptly that the boy had to let go of his fork and drop it onto the plate to avoid splattering syrup across his grandfather's shoulder. Poppa turned in a quick circle, spinning with Damon in his arms in the kitchen and laughing a laugh that was all things joyful. It was a laugh of pride and delight, surprise and wonder. He said, "That's the way it's done, Damon! That's my boy! Did you two hear that?"

In any other family a grandfather would react that way to the boy's first words, to his first sentence, perhaps to his first touch down. "That was pure Damon, people!" Poppa announced. "It was. Wasn't it?" The question came with a complete stop in the action. It was an urgent interruption of the spinning, laughing celebration.

Damon nodded into his grandfather's shoulder and said, "I just thought of it. Just now."

"Well done," Dad said gruffly and sounded just a little bit annoyed when he said it.

That did nothing to diminish the moment for Damon, though. He was wrapped in his grandfather's arms, receiving and relishing the reward for his effort. The hug was part of it, the joy, the appreciation. But the best of it, the biggest part, the thing that stirred his heart and set him on his path, the thing that told him above all else that he had done something good and right and wonderful was the laughter.

Then Leonard came in with his baseball glove and found a way to suck the life out of the room.

1984

"This is maybe the hardest thing about comedy, Damon."

"What about knowing when to get off stage?"

"That too," Poppa said. "But this, this is   always hard. There's a lot going on. There's a whole world of bullshit. Club owners that jerk you around for your money, they think it's easier to rip you off if you're never sure you had a good show. Hecklers who're too drunk to know they're not part of the show. Waitresses doing their jobs, sirens going by, all sorts of shit. Some nights you're gonna have a crappy night, go down in flames. Only people laughing are the comics in the back who hate your guts and want to see you squirm. None of it matters, kid. You hold on to the victory. You know what I'm saying?"

"Sort of."

"Ed's fuckin' wine, Kid. That's what I'm saying. You got suspended. So what? You lost your place during your act. So what? Ed's fucking wine, see ball-point pen offer on back. You were a winner the night you wrote that joke."

1994

Damon looked out at the cloudscape that spread out below him now. He tapped on the window with the edge of his metal splint. He thought ahead to the airport a bit, to Cynthia picking him up, to the ride home. Maybe he had done as well as Matthew had said. Maybe he had just gotten himself booked on

Letterman and maybe he would be able to make the jump to headliner at all the clubs in the country now.

Maybe it was a meaningless conversation. Maybe it was a showbiz blow-off. He wouldn't know for a while. He couldn't know yet whether it was a yes that meant "yes" or the yes that comes at the start of yes-plus-time-equals-no. He was beginning to learn something his father had told him a long time ago, that it is only possible to know the meaning of events after some time has passed, when they can be looked back on in context.

For now, though, he had one thing to hold on to as he raced home at the speed of flight. One thing that he knew he had gained on this trip. He picked up his thin Styrofoam cup full of bad airline coffee and muttered to himself, "Hulk sip."

CHAPTER TEN

2004

Damon unlocked the door and held it open so that Cynthia could race past him to the bathroom. She had announced her need to pee just as they got on the 101 North, a few moments before they found that the freeway was running at the speed of a four-star restaurant's drive-thru window.

Cynthia's rush was such that she entirely failed to notice that someone was in their house waiting for them. Damon stood just inside the doorway gazing, stunned at the unexpected visitor. He considered making a threatening move to cause a swift departure, but he didn't want to risk being attacked. Instead, he said very calmly, very off-handedly, "Hello."

From the bathroom, Cynthia shouted, "Did you say something?"

The visitor did not say anything. The visitor, sitting comfortably in the very center of the dining table, lifted a leg like a life-long yogi, stretched downward with a face of indeterminate age and licked its own ass.

"There's a cat," Damon told her.

"Wait. I can't hear you. The fan." Cynthia said.

A few moments later, she emerged from the bathroom, fastening her jeans, to learn that, indeed, there was a cat.

"Any idea where it came from?" Damon asked.

"The bathroom window was open a crack. Maybe it squeezed through."

1977

Poppa sat with Damon on a fallen log and tossed bits of bread into the water. They watched the ducks snatch the soggy mouthfuls and circle back, hoping always for a bit more.

Poppa made a sound like a duck at them. They were already swimming close. Damon had heard him make this sound his whole life. Every time he'd come to visit the old man, they had sat out here and fed the ducks and his grandfather had made that sound. He had always thought it was supposed to call the ducks to them, but now he realized that it was just something Poppa did. He was conversing with the ducks a little bit. He quacked and they quacked. He was also showing off his ability to make a sound like a duck.

Damon smiled. He tapped the side of his cheek and then pushed a light whistle out with his tongue to create the short-rising "plunk" of a water drop.

Poppa turned to him, a bit surprised. "That was a good one. Do that one again."

Damon made the sound.

"You have to teach me that some day," Poppa said. Then he quacked.

Damon plunked.

They tossed bread on the water.

After a long span of quiet, Poppa said, "Your

mother wants me to talk to you."

"You don't want to?"

Poppa laughed. "I always want to talk to you. But there are some things I'm supposed to tell you now that I wouldn't always think of telling you on my own."

"Why can't she tell me?"

"She knows this is the sort of thing I should tell you."

Then there was another long silence and Poppa didn't tell him anything.

"I love these ducks. I been feeding these ducks for forty years now."

"They don't look that old," Damon said.

Poppa grinned at him. "I used to have a cat. This was before you were born. It used to come out here with me and watch me feed the ducks. Made him crazy at first. He wanted to kill a duck, but he didn't want to go in the water. Then he figured out it was nice just to sit in the sun with me. He'd lie and watch the ducks. Then, one day, big, stupid, friendly duck came up out of the water to get bread and that cat just sniffed at it and let it be. For a whole summer those two sat with me out here, the duck and the cat and me."

"You're kidding me, right?"

"No. You'll be able to tell. When I kid you, there'll be humor content."

Damon grinned at him. "Mom didn't want you to tell me about cats and ducks, Poppa."

"No. No she didn't."

"Is this about school?"

"The suspension?"

"Yeah."

"Partly."

They sat for a while longer, tossing bread, watching ducks.

"A while back, Leonard beat the crap out of you."

"He was being an idiot."

"He said you were making fun of him, but that's not how you told it."

"Yeah. That was . . . a while ago. It doesn't matter."

"It does. It matters. You got suspended from school for talking back. But you and I both know that's not how you were thinking of it."

"Poppa, I'm not sure I know what we're talking about."

"You were making a joke, weren't you? At school. With Leonard. It was the same thing. There was a joke and you couldn't let it go."

Damon looked down at his sneakers for a moment. He made patterns in the dirt with the waffled sole of one of them, then turned his foot to make an intersecting grid pattern.

"You mom wants me to tell you that there are times when it's not appropriate to make a joke. There are times when you just have to let a joke go untold, a thought go unsaid."

"Okay. You've told me."

"No. No, I haven't. And I'm not going to. I'm going to tell you something else entirely."

Now Poppa had his grandson's full attention.

"Damon, you have to decide, every time, whether you're willing to face the consequences when you tell a joke. Every time. A good joke, any good joke, it tells the truth. They're very powerful and they can hurt people and they can change the world. I am not   being funny with you. I am not playing around. A lot of people, most people have no idea what kind of power there is in a joke. Even people who make their living telling them, a lot of them have no clue. I'm telling you. 'Cause you get it. You get how jokes work. You get what they are. You need to have the tools to—" Poppa searched for exactly the right words. Poppa almost never had to stop to search for words. He went on. "You need to be able to take responsibility for what you can do. You have the ability to change the way people think. You have the ability to say things that will hang with a person forever, change the way they see the whole world."

Damon took that in. "Change the way they see the whole world." He said softly, thinking about superpowers and responsibility and Spiderman.

Poppa said, "Hey! Is there a gecko in here?"

Damon blinked, amazed that his grandfather remembered his joke from so long ago.

2004

"Stanley Myron Handlecat," Damon said.

"Henny Youngcat," Cynthia said.

"Willie Locat," Damon said.

"M. Furry Abraham," Cynthia said.

The cat sat back on its big cat ass, rested its front legs on the inside of its thighs so that it appeared to be lounging in a deck chair and said, with clarity and diction, "Wow."

"M. Furry Abraham it is!" Damon said.

"We should buy a litter box," Cynthia said.

CHAPTER ELEVEN

2004

Matthew said something that was interrupted several times by the bleeping and blooping of touch tones. Then he said, "What the hell?"

"Sorry," Damon said. "M. Furry Abraham doesn't like it when I talk on the phone at my desk."

Damon lifted the cat into his lap and scratched under his chin. Matthew repeated the information.

"Okay," Damon said. "That sounds good to me. Accept the gig and e-mail me all the information, would you?"

He listened to the exact rant he had anticipated and then said, "Stop bitching at me and e-mail it. I can't write or type anything right now 'cause I have a huge cat in my lap who needs to be controlled if we want to have an uninterrupted conversation."

He shouted to Cynthia. "I'm headlining the Bahia in San Diego the weekend of the 23rd. You wanna come down with me?"

1994

"Are you serious?" Damon pretended disbelief, hoping to mask his anger, his sadness.

"Please don't be mad," Matthew said.

Cynthia said, "It's a week at a resort, Damon.

You love the Bahia."

"I'm the feature act for Louie Drucker. Really? Eight hundred bucks and I'm a feature act for a man who wears fuzzy antlers through half of his show?"

"Drucker's been headlining there for fifteen years. He's a name. You know how it works."

"I thought I knew how it works. I thought you told me how it works. Letterman was the key, you said. Then I could headline anywhere. Did I suck? Did I bomb on national television and nobody told me? What the hell, Matthew?"

"You did great. But it's over. The boom. It's over. In the last six months we've had—what?—eight, nine hundred venues close down around the country. Not just one-nighters in sports bars, Man. We're talkin' about actual clubs. Albuquerque, Tempe, Redding, gone. Johnny B's in Utah, gone. The—what was that place in Park City?—Gone. I'm getting you every gig I can, but the clubs just aren't there and the ones that are there aren't bumping up the feature acts the way they were."

Damon put his head in his hands and tried not to yell at his friend for things that he knew were not Matthew's fault.

"I'll come down with you," Cynthia said. "It'll be fun."

"If you don't want to do it, just say so. I'll tell them to find someone else," Matthew offered.

1992

Damon sat at the Daily Grill franchise at LAX and watched his father sip scotch from a glass.

"I just don't understand what you're doing out here," Dad said. "I'm not saying you're not doing something, or that I disapprove. I'm just saying that I don't understand it. I don't understand . . ." he thought for a long moment, trying to choose the right words or perhaps trying to edit the wrong ones. Then he said, "I don't understand what it is that you hope to accomplish."

"I'm a comic, Dad. I hope to accomplish wealth and fame and the adoration of strangers."

Dad snorted a snort that said, "Those are not real goals," and "I understand that you're being flip about this and that is not really all you hope to accomplish." He said, "If that's what you want, you can do it as a writer. Do you remember the stories you used to write?"

"I do. I still write stories sometimes."

"They were so beautiful. You wrote one . . . I still remember it. About a woman who thinks it's always raining and then she slowly realizes that she never thinks about going outdoors when the sun is shining. Do you know what I'm talking about?"

"I do. Yeah. I remember that story, Dad. I didn't write that story. I told you about that story. My friend Katherine wrote that story and I told you about it because I was afraid I'd never be able to write anything that hung with anybody over time the way that story hung with me."

Dad was silent for a long, shameful moment before he said, "But you did write beautiful stories. You won those awards and you were always at that typewriter. Do you remember that typewriter? Your mother and I gave it to you for your fourteenth birthday."

"I do remember the typewriter."

"Whatever happened to that typewriter?"

"I used tin foil and plumbing supplies to turn it into a bong."

Dad snorted.

"I still have it," Damon said. "I still use it."

"You should call your brother," Dad said.

"Leonard doesn't like me very much," Damon told him.

"He's still angry."

"I don't see why. It wasn't *his* funeral."

Dad snorted, a little bit harshly.

"Besides, it didn't even turn out to be the funniest part of the thing," Damon added.

Dad snorted again, a more wholehearted sort of a snort.

1985

The dense gathering at the gravesite made Damon suddenly aware of just how many people had loved his grandfather. His father brushed a bit of snow and left-over schmutz from the back of his coat with a slapping gesture that seemed to be as much a terse warning as an act of grooming and affection.

The contact was both harsh and loving. It implied that he knew Damon was still angry with his brother, but that he would not tolerate any lashing out at this time.

Four men, employees of the facility, lowered Poppa's casket into the ground slowly. Mom cried, whimpering softly. There were quiet sniffles and left-over chuckles from the events back at the synagogue. There was no wailing, though. No weeping. No rending of garments. No beating of breasts.

One at a time, members of the group stepped forward, each dropping a handful of dirt into the hole, offering up a moment's thought, a whispered word. Each moved past the family members speaking soft remembrance, condolence, kindness.

Then, not knowing quite what came next, they returned to their positions around the gravesite. A huge, yellow, rumbling bulldozer climbed the small rise and began pushing the remaining pile of earth into the hole. The appearance of the heavy equipment seemed incongruous, utterly inappropriate to the solemnity of the occasion. After each plowing pass, it backed up, beeping the same beep made by garbage trucks and delivery vehicles.

Everyone knew at once that something had gone wrong with the ceremonial planning. Surely there ought to have been some signal, some moment at which everyone walked away in silence back to their cars before the burial became nothing more than a pot-holing operation. Certainly this was not how normal funerals ended. The viewing of the body, the words of sorrow and memory, the slow processional of vehicles behind the hearse and then the beeping and roaring of a public works project.

Now, though, there seemed to be no way of escaping, no appropriate way of walking off until the whole task was complete. The funeral gathering remained in place like a group of overdressed union foremen. The longer it went on, the harder it became for Damon to keep from laughing.

1992

Dad checked his watch and although he still had half an hour left on his layover he said, "I should probably get to the gate."

"Okay," Damon said.

Neither of them got up to move.

"You know I had to do it, right?"

"You've told me."

"I didn't have a choice."

"Damon, don't do that."

"What am I doing?"

"You did what you did. You *chose* to do what you did. You made a decision. You went to his funeral with a plan in place to get a laugh. Maybe you thought it was a special way to honor him. Maybe you're just that pathetically addicted to the sound of laughter. I don't know why. I may never know why. But don't make it sound like it was out of your control. You did what you did. You had a choice."

Damon nodded. He shrugged. "Yeah."

"You went for the laugh. You didn't care what it did to anybody else. All you cared about was going for the laugh."

"You know what Poppa always used to say."

"Yes. Yes, I do. But the fact that he used to say it, doesn't mean he was right."

That was a thought that rocked Damon back a bit. That was something that had never occurred to him at all.

1974

Leonard appeared in the doorway of the kitchen holding his baseball mitt. He wore the uniform of his little league team. "You know the game's at eleven. Right?"

"We'll be there, Buddy," Dad said. He glanced at his watch to be sure that he had as much time to smoke and do the crossword puzzle as he had thought.

"Okay," Leonard said. He became aware of the grins passing between Poppa and Damon, and knew that he had missed something. He asked, "What's going on?"

"Damon wrote a joke," Mom said. "That's all."

Light shone more brightly in the smiles shared by Damon and Poppa then. They knew that there was nothing "all" about it. They both knew that it was a big, big deal.

"Whattaya mean?" Leonard asked.

"I don't understand the question," Dad said.

Poppa spoke up. "Your brother just wrote his first joke."

"I don't get it. What is that? 'Wrote a joke?' You mean, like, he wrote down a joke? Or he made one up?"

"I made one up," Damon said.

"Let's hear it." Leonard said, but it was a challenge, not a real request.

"Okay," Damon said.

Before he could go any further, Poppa interrupted him. "Do it with me."

"What?" Damon asked.

"I'll do the straight man."

"The what?" Damon said.

"The straight man. You don't know what a straight man is?"

Damon shook his head. Poppa turned to Leonard and said, "You go to practice. We'll see you at game time. You can hear the joke another time. There are things I need to tell your brother."

Leonard rolled his eyes and let out the sigh that has always been the exclusive expression of the adolescent. He let out the exhausted, disdainful sigh that says, "Everybody other than me is a complete moron and I can't even believe I have to share a planet with them." He walked out of the kitchen leaving behind him a sense of sadness and guilt in his parents, a sense of irritability in his grandfather and a sense of disappointment in young Damon.

"What was that about?" Damon asked.

"That's how teenagers are, Damon," Dad said.

"That's not what he meant," Poppa said.

Damon confirmed his grandfather's assertion. "Why didn't you let me tell him the joke?"

"Never tell a joke to someone whose attitude says, 'I bet you can't make me laugh.' It only leads to heartbreak."

Damon took in the information and thought about it. He let it sink deep into his consciousness as he did all the information Poppa offered him about jokes and laughter. Poppa knew everything about jokes. He knew how they worked, he knew how to make them better, he knew how important they could be. Poppa had been a comedian a long time ago and Damon wanted to know everything his grandfather had ever learned. He wanted to know everything his grandfather could teach him.

1992

Dad drank the last of his scotch and signaled the waitress for a refill, now committed to a little more time sitting with his son.

"You really never thought of that, did you?" Simon asked.

Poppa could have been wrong. No. No, he really had never thought of that at all. He felt the information trying to sink in and he felt himself fighting the idea. It seemed stupid, but the thought made him a little bit dizzy. He shook his head.

"Wow, kiddo. If it's hitting you this hard to find out that Poppa was mortal, what's it going to do to you when you realize that I'm only human, too?"

"Oh, Dad," Damon said. "The ship sailed on that discovery a long, long time ago."

Dad snorted a snort that said, "Well played," and "Nicely phrased" and also, "See? You should be writing stories and books, Damon, not putting together little jokes to tell on stage."

1994

"Of course I want the gig," Damon said, the anger draining away.

"Oh good!" Cynthia said and both Damon and Matthew knew it was because she loved the resort and wanted the excuse to go there with Damon.

"I'll book it then," Matthew said.

Cynthia said, "Get us a room where I can look out and see the seals, would you?"

Matthew laughed. "There's a contract rider you don't hear about."

2004

"Nice!" Cynthia shouted back and then she ran up the stairs to stand in the doorway of Damon's office.

Damon released M. Furry Abraham. The cat remained in his lap, sprawled like a drunk nudist, privates exposed to the cool breeze of the ceiling fan.

"Did they give us our room again?"

"But of course," Damon said. "Matthew said that when he booked it in they asked if 'the wife who likes the seals' would be coming."

"That doesn't mean they remember me. It just means they take notes on the people who stay there."

"Wow," Damon said. "Are you really going to dismiss the pleasure of being remembered as an individual as casually as that?"

"I am," Cynthia said.

"Wow," M. Furry Abraham said.

"Don't you start with me," Cynthia said. Then she said, "Do you want to come to San Diego with us? You can see seals from our room."

CHAPTER TWELVE

2004

Damon wandered from the room out to the comedy club in the early afternoon just to check out the space. He'd been there many times before, but he tried to stay on top of the basics, making sure the mic stand was in good shape, shaking hands with the room's manager, that sort of thing.

Cynthia remained behind, looking out through the window at the seals in their little pool with the fountain at the center. The seals slept, as they did frequently, on their favorite sunning rocks. As Damon walked past them, he turned toward the hotel and waved up at the window. He could dimly make out Cynthia's form as she waved back.

He made his way into the club and let his eyes adjust from the bright San Diego sun to the dim lighting of the room.

An older woman sat at the bar sipping something through a tiny stir-straw. The bartender seemed to have stepped away, probably to a back room where work needed to be done during the day when people were unlikely to be in the club drinking. Damon stepped up to the bar as he scanned the room, noticing the tripod-based mic stand on the stage.

He said, "Is there anyone working here?"

The woman said, "Kid brought me this drink,

didn't he?"

"I'm guessing he did," Damon said.

There was a short pause then before the woman said, "You, sir, are an alcoholic."

"Really, not." Damon told her.

"Denial," she announced, "is the first symptom."

"Fair enough," Damon said. "Maybe I'm an alcoholic. I can't tell. I never drink enough to find out."

The woman chuckled at that.

Walking into a comedy club in the afternoon always held a sense of melancholy for Damon. The empty tables and unlit candles had the underweighted feel of stage props, the white, plastic skull which, when lifted, could not possibly ever have been Yorik, the chrome-painted wooden sword that posed no threat at all.

1983

Damon entered the IMPROV just a little bit out of breath. He had run from the subway as though it made a difference whether he arrived for his set five hours and ten minutes early or five hours and fourteen minutes early. The show hadn't started yet. The earliest audience members still clustered at the bar, while waitresses in the showroom lit candles and placed logo-printed matchbooks in freshly wiped ashtrays.

The club's owner gestured for Damon to meet her in the room and disappeared. He followed eagerly, thinking he might be bumped up from "developing regular" to "regular." He imagined he might be   put on the coveted weekend lineup. He imagined that perhaps she had someone special coming in to see the show tonight, someone for whom she wanted him to showcase. He imagined, as he always did in one way or another, that tonight's show was somehow going to change his life, skyrocket him to sudden celebrity.

He walked into the show room and saw it, for the first time, under the revealing incandescence of the work lights and the house lights. The room that had always been so full of magic and possibility, the room that had always been a glamorous cavern echoing with the laughter of dimly visible spirits was now nothing more than a place of business. Any bar, jazz joint or strip club would have looked the same. Stains on the table cloths, invisible in the audience's darkness, showed cheaply under the bright bulbs. Chips in the glass candleholders, high-traffic areas of the painted floor worn through to bare cement, even the single rail of stage lights exposed the place for what it was, a cheap nightclub dedicated to collecting covers and selling drinks.

Damon felt his heart sink in a way that was shockingly familiar and he knew at once when he had felt it before.

1975

Damon and Poppa stood just inside the entrance to the carnival. Damon smelled the sweet air. Fried dough dipped in confectioner's sugar, cotton candy, bubble gum and spilled soda filled each breath with the promise of delicious reward. Bells and snippets of music reached his ears over the enthusiastic calls of carnies inviting contestants to play their games, celebrating the winners, empathizing with the losers in exactly the same practiced tones.

Poppa bent down, crouching beside Damon and said, "Take it in. Don't let it take you in. Listen and watch for a second 'cause once we walk into that mess it's gonna be hard to think. You understand?"

Damon said, "Uh-huh." But he did not understand at all.

"What order do you want to do this in?" Poppa asked him. "Do we start by playing games and riding rides and then get to the lesson, or do we start with the lesson?"

Damon was eleven years old. Damon did not opt for delayed gratification. It was, perhaps, the wisest choice he had ever made.

For an hour and a half, as the sun moved higher into the sky, Damon tossed rings at bottles to win small toys. He squirted water at a target to trigger an air tank that filled a balloon much too slowly. The man running the booth tousled his hair and called him "son". He rode the tilt-a-whirl and the octopus and the Ferris Wheel. He looked at himself in distorting mirrors and stumbled through a funhouse where the floors tilted at odd angles and mannequins jumped at him in black-light face-paint. He ate a hot dog with mustard and ketchup and sauerkraut. He carried a balloon until it slipped from his fingers.

When he was just starting to get tired of the whole affair, but had not yet noticed the waning of his own interest, Poppa said, "Now. Are you ready never to see a fair the same way again?"

Damon did not know what that meant, but Poppa seemed very excited, bubbling with anticipation. Damon said, "Okay."

Poppa led him past the long row of gaming booths until they'd nearly reached the far end of the fair grounds. Poppa held his hand tightly and he did not bend down as he spoke to Damon, now. That made Damon feel very much as though he was being treated as an equal, spoken to as an adult, a temporarily short adult.

Poppa said, "You may be too young for this. I'm not sure. But I think you're ready. It's hard always to know."

"I'm ready," Damon said. He did not know what was going on, and he was a little bit nervous, but he loved his grandfather and he wanted very much not to let him down by not being ready.

They came to a narrow gap between two booths and Poppa led him through it. The moment they entered the alley, the sound of the carnival diminished, muffled by layers of canvas and plywood. Ten steps, maybe fewer, and they emerged behind the hastily constructed booths.

Lengths of rope ran from cloth booth tops to iron spikes hammered into the ground. Huge metal trash barrels overflowed with cardboard boxes and discarded Styrofoam. Coffee cups littered the ground and empty TV dinner foils. Carnival workers, their hands dirty and their faces streaked with sweat, sat on plastic crates and smoked cigarettes. Two men shared a drink from a bottle wrapped in a brown paper bag. A voice shouted, "What're you doing back here?" The voice was angry, threatening even. Damon looked up to see that it was the man from the squirt-gun booth. The man who had called him "son" and smiled at him when he lost. He walked toward them as though he meant to physically escort them back the way they'd come.

Poppa said, "Settle down. I'm Alvie Grunman. I'm showing my grandson the ropes."

Showing him the ropes, Damon thought, believing he had just learned the true meaning of a phrase he'd heard all his life. He looked at the worn, rough ropes, stained and smeared with grease and filth. He noticed the filth on the carny's hands and wondered if they'd been that dirty when the man had touched his hair. He found he suddenly wanted a shower very, very badly.

Poppa moved forward, away from Damon, extending a hand to the man, Damon did not want his grandfather to touch the man's sooty paw as he reached out to shake Poppa's hand. While they spoke quietly, the boy took in these new surroundings.

If he tried, he could still make out the carnival sounds, but they were quite distant. Traffic from a nearby street was far more audible and when a truck went by, it shook the earth and drowned out the music and the barkers entirely. The smells back here were of garbage and while they were still laced with the sugary sweetness of jelly beans and rock candy, they carried a sickliness in them that filled Damon with an odd sort of longing, a sense of loss, of illusions shattered and magic tricks demystified. The ropes that held the place erect were rough and sinewy, and the canvas booth backs were smudged, stained and worn from use and reuse.

Poppa moved away from the man now, back toward Damon, ushering him back through the   alleyway as the man shouted, ". . . Don't care! Nobody comes back here!" Damon tripped over a cardboard tray full of big stuffed animal prizes, protected under a shrink-wrap cover. He looked back to see what had caught his foot and saw that the plastic was coated with dust and sand. The prizes waiting to be arranged on shelves and given out to visitors were barely distinguishable from the trash that littered the ground. The full box looked exactly as valued and valuable as the empty ones.

Abruptly, they stepped back into the world of the fair. Damon looked at it with new eyes, now. He heard the words in his head again. *Nobody comes back here.* He looked at all the people, smiling, some tired and still ready to try another ride, another game. None of them had gone through the alleyway. None of them knew how filthy it all was, how fake. None of them knew how quickly the music would fade, how lumpy the prizes looked, packaged under plastic.

Only he knew that. He knew and his grandfather knew and the people who worked the booths and the rides knew. He also knew that he could never look at it all the same way again, that he could never just enjoy the colors and the smells the way he had just minutes earlier.

It made him sad. It made him want to weep. It also made him feel very, very special.

1983

The owner of the Improv gestured to Damon, inviting him to join her at a back table in the club. Waitresses lit candles up near the stage, straightened chairs, got the place ready to look deceptively glamorous.

Damon sat down with her.

"You're not performing tonight," she told him.

"What?"

"Suspended. Two weeks."

"You can suspend me?"

"I can fire you if I want. I own the club."

"Right. But. I mean. Why? Not 'why do you own the club.' Why are you suspending me? What does that even mean?"

"It means don't bother calling in for spots for the next two weeks. And when you start coming in again, you don't make fun of the food. You understand?"

"What? When did I make fun of the food?"

"Last Thursday. You think if I'm not here, people don't tell me what went on in the room?"

"I made fun of the . . .?" Then he remembered. "That was *improvised*." He said. "I didn't even realize how funny it was until I'd said it and the room was laughing."

"You can't keep your head about you, don't engage the audience. Someone offers you something on stage, you accept it graciously and you pretend to enjoy it. You understand me?"

Damon nodded, stunned, numb.

"You know what you do *not* do?"

"I don't make fun of the food?"

"You don't make fun of the food."

Damon nodded and stood up to go, to get back on the subway and then back on the train out to his parents' house. Before he reached the door, though, she said, "And Damon?" So he stopped to hear what else she had to say. "When you get back I'm gonna try you out in some prime-time spots. That was a pretty funny line you said to the guy."

"What guy?" Damon asked.

"The guy with the fried zucchini. 'No thanks. I've eaten here.' That's funny. You got good instincts, kid."

Damon nodded. "Um . . . thanks?" he said. Then he left the club and for the first time ever he understood the meaning of the phrase 'profound ambivalence.'

2004

The bartender, clean shaven and white-shirted, looked a bit relieved to see somebody other than the accusatory old woman at the bar as he came back into the room. He smiled warmly at Damon, his eyes hinting at desperation and hope for salvation.

"Hi," Damon said. "Is Jacob still running things around here?"

"He'll be in at four or so to start setting up. Can I get you anything?"

"You can get me a round-based mic stand," he said. "I'm Damon Blazer. I'm headlining tonight. You gonna be working the bar during the show?"

"All night long," the bartender said.

"Okay, good," Damon said. "Here's the thing."

1982

Poppa took a deep breath through his nose and the oxygen tubes hissed in response.

"You okay?" Damon said.

"Yeah. I'm great. This is a daring fashion choice." He pushed at the tube with the back of his hand to indicate what it was that he was claiming as an accessory.

"So . . . I think I made a mistake. I mean . . . not a bad one. Just, I wanted to ask you about it."

"You kill someone?"

"What? No. Poppa, why would you say that?"

"I want you to know whatever it is I'm okay to tell it to. Unless you had sex with an old man. I don't care if you're gay, but if you're having sex with old men, that would make me uncomfortable."

"Really?"

"Yeah. 'Cause, in case you haven't noticed, as old men go, I'm quite a looker."

"Okay, Poppa."

"And I'm your grandfather. So that would make me uncomfortable."

"Are you gonna let me tell you this or are you going to keep talking until your heart stops?"

"Hah! So now you DO think I'm gonna die."

"I got annoyed with a guy . . . not a heckler, really. Just a guy in the crowd. Kept laughing and yell-ing, 'That's great!' every time he liked a joke."

"That's still heckling. It feels different, but it's the same damn thing. Fucking hecklers. They throw you off your game, they mess up your show and they think they're helping. Always a heckler comes up to you after the show wants to shake your hand. I fucking hate them."

"I know, Poppa. But this was different. He wasn't—you know—'You suck!' or whatever. You don't want to come down hard on someone who keeps saying you're great. You know? So I said, 'You like me so much, why don't you buy me a drink?'"

"Was this an old guy? 'Cause now I'm starting to think I was right with the whole—"

"Poppa. Please. Listen."

"Okay. Sorry, kid. Tell me."

"I thought it was a funny line, but next thing I know, the waitress comes up to me with a shot of scotch on the stage. And the crowd starts chanting for me to do the shot and I don't want to say that I'm not old enough to drink in the club, so I downed the shot, right there. On stage."

Poppa laughed. "Did you throw up?"

"No. But I could tell my words got a little bit slurred, like, right away. They all cheered and laughed and applauded and I did some pretty funny shit after that but still . . . I didn't like it. I felt a little bit out of control. I did a thing . . ." He trailed off and Poppa became suddenly worried.

"Oh." Poppa said.

"What?"

"This isn't about drinking on stage. This is something else. Isn't it?"

"What do you mean?"

"All right. Listen kid. You think it might happen again—and it might—sometimes people want to buy a drink for the comic—you go to the bartender every time before the show. Tell him if anyone orders you a drink, he puts apple juice in a shot glass or over ice. Looks just like scotch. Put scotch on their bill. Nobody's the wiser and you get to look like you can hold your liquor like nobody's business. You get it?"

Damon nodded.

"But that's not what you want to talk to me about. That's not your question. Something happened after you drank the scotch. Something on stage."

Damon nodded. He didn't know what had given him away, didn't know how his grandfather could have figured that out, but it was exactly right.

Poppa said, "What? Were you funnier than you're used to being? You afraid you're gonna start wanting to drink before you—?"

"No," Damon cut him off. "No. That's not it, Poppa. I'm sorry. I'm sorry." It was a wave of sadness, of apology, of regret bursting out of him, purging itself in a sudden torrent of tears and snot. He grabbed a Kleenex from the box beside Poppa's bed.

"What the hell, Kid? You gotta tell me more now, 'cause I don't know what the hell this is about. Jesus. You sure you didn't kill someone?"

Damon shook his head, weeping.

"And you're sure you didn't sleep with an old guy?"

Damon chuckled while he cried. "I did a joke about you. I wrote it a while ago and it made me nervous, so I didn't do it. But then . . . I had this shot of scotch and I was saying anything   that crossed my mind and it just came out. I'm so sorry."

"You did a joke about me?"

"Yeah."

"Did it get laughs?"

"Uh-huh."

"So . . . what's the problem?"

Damon said nothing.

"What was the joke?" Poppa asked gently.

Damon took a deep breath. "My grandfather has Alzheimer's. The last time I visited, it was ridiculous. Every time he saw me he thought it was my birthday and gave me five dollars. Just exhausting to deal with. I had to keep walking in and out of that room."

Poppa laughed. "Damon, it's a good joke."

"You're not upset?"

"What do I always say, Kid?"

"Really?"

"What do I always say? Say it for me. Say it aloud. Now. Say it."

"Comedy First."

"Uh-huh," Poppa encouraged him.

"Safety second."

"That's right. Keep going."

"Other people's feelings last."

"Good boy. Say it again. Say it with me."

They recited the creed together, like boy scouts doing the pledge of allegiance. "Comedy first. Safety second. Other people's feelings last."

"Good. Now you remember that, when it's time to keep your promise. Okay?"

Damon looked down at the brown paper bag, still clutched in his hand. With all the crying and the shameful confessing, he had sweated up the paper and crumpled the mouth of the bag into a wrinkled mess.

2004

"Wait," the bartender said. "What?"

"I'm saying you charge them for the scotch, but you give me apple juice. That way I don't get drunk on stage and they feel good about buying me a drink."

"Is that even legal?"

"I have no idea," Damon said. "Never occurred to me. Just do it."

CHAPTER THIRTEEN

2004

Damon came back into the room to find Cynthia on the phone. She grinned at him, a silly, happy grin. He had no idea what it could possibly mean. She held a finger up at him, signaling him to wait while she listened. She responded with occasional "Uh-huhs".

Whatever the conversation was about, it clearly made her happy. She shifted her weight from left to right in a little dance of excitement. Damon watched her, fighting the urge to blurt out questions, to demand inclusion.

1994

Matthew did a goofy little dance in the middle of the living room, surrounded by half-emptied boxes. The boxes had been placed in the general area appropriate to their contents. It seemed to Damon as though memories of the old apartment had already begun to spill out into this new place.

Matthew held the receiver to his ear and gestured frantically to Damon to write down what he was saying, like a diner signaling for a check. Damon gestured at the chaos surrounding him to let Matthew know that the odds of him finding a writing implement and scratch pad were very slim.

Cynthia tore a top-flap from a box and grabbed a magic marker that she'd used days earlier to mark boxes for placement in particular rooms. She nodded to Matthew.

Damon noticed with an odd sort of specificity of focus that the edge of the torn cardboard looked like a map of the Texas/Mexico border.

1972

Damon felt the rough texture of the wood grain beneath his finger tips.

He looked at the difference in size between his own feet and his father's.

He imitated his father's posture, resting elbows on knees as they sat side by side on the steps in front of the house in Turdoc.

Dad said, "Damon, some people think the truth is a malleable thing, that if they just believe something strongly enough, it will become true. Even if they just pretend to believe something strongly enough." He unrolled the comic book, turned it over, rolled it back up with the front facing outward this time.

"You, father," Damon said in a mock-British accent, "are a killer of Tinkerbell!"

Dad snorted, "Funny," and also, "You understand more than I expect you to," and also, "Good. This point is made. We can move on." He said, "The idea that you might be able to be hypnotized into knowing the future through some sort of freed intuition is a kind of magical thinking. We may perceive more than we're aware of most of the time, but that doesn't mean we're masking some sort of prescience."

"Prescience again. What is that?"

"The ability to know the future is prescience."

"Ah."

"Knowledge of right and wrong is conscience. Knowledge of everything is omniscience."

"Got it. And you don't think we could unlock that through hypnosis?"

"I think that's a nice idea for a science-fiction story or a comic book, but no. I don't think it could really happen."

Damon nodded.

Dad went on. "Most of the time, Damon, we don't even know most of what's happening right this minute. Not just what's happening far away or behind our backs or what-have-you. Right now. We're constantly noticing things, picking things up from our surroundings, details that catch our eyes for no apparent reason, that turn out to be the really important thing that happened while we were involved in something else entirely. It's only in retrospect that we can really sort out what was important and what wasn't."

"Retrospect?"

"Hindsight."

"Ah."

"Introspection is looking inward. Inspection is looking closely."

"So, a close inspection is redundant?"

Dad snorted, but it was an empty snort, just to fill the space in the conversation. There were no three or four things he wanted to say behind it. "Most of what happens is just coming at us too fast to make any sort of sense at all," Dad said. "It's a disjointed mess. You take a train. There's a guy with red sneakers. You get married. You have a kid—"

"Not necessarily in that order," Damon said.

"Fair enough," Dad said with a genuine chuckle. "Let me give you an example. About a year after your mother and I were married, she got sick. It turned out it was just food poisoning, but I didn't know. She had a fever; she was shivering, throwing up. I rushed her to the hospital. They took her away to run tests to figure out what it was. I'm pacing back and forth, waiting, nervous, 'is she going to be okay?' There's a woman in the waiting room with me. She's got this big gold wedding ring, thick, looks like a man's ring and she's got it around her thumb. She keeps turning the ring on her thumb with the fingers of her other hand. I notice it, don't really pay attention. I overhear her talking to the doctor about her father. He's just had a stroke, not a bad one, wait-and-see if there's any lasting paralysis, that sort of thing. You with me?"

"Um," Damon said.

Dad said, "Five years later, I'm up for a job at Princeton in the English Department. This is a big jump for me if I get it, going from an associate professorship to full professor. A better school than the one I've been at. I want this to happen. I have a meeting with the department head. She's vaguely familiar. I can't figure out why. Then I notice this huge gold ring on her thumb and I remember why I know her. I tell her about sitting in the waiting room with her that day. She tells me about her father, how he recovered and then died three years later in a car accident that she thinks might've been another stroke. We have this great, human connection and I wind up with the Princeton position. Now, some people would say there was the hand of destiny at work, giving me the cues years earlier that I would need to land the job. Some people would say 'god' or 'fate' or some damn thing because people are hard-wired to look for pattern, to seek out cause-and-effect relationships even where none exist. On the other hand, I also remember, when I was in that hospital waiting room, seeing a framed instructional poster on how to tell the difference between a cold and a flu. I remember that the corner of the frame was chipped and I remember there was a typo on this mass-produced poster saying that if no fever was present you were likely to have caught a common cod. There's no reason to assume, because of that, that someday I would be meeting the guy who framed the poster, or interview for a job proofreading hospital instructional materials . . ."

"Or get sick while fishing in Nantucket," Damon put in.

Dad sighed. "I'm making a point here,   Damon. Everything doesn't have to be turned into a joke."

"No," Damon said. "But everything *can* be."

Damon thought about his half-conscious awareness of the wood grain beneath his fingertips. He thought about the moment he had spent contemplating relative shoe sizes. He wondered what the important part of this event had been. What element or elements he would remember. Whether any of the conversation would ever bear any relevance other than to destroy his belief in the possibility of prescience.

Dad said, "Is any of this making sense to you? Do you have any questions or . . ." he trailed off.

Damon said, "Just one."

"What's that?"

"After you killed Tinkerbell did you bury her with Santa Claus and the Easter Bunny?"

Dad snorted and his snort had many, many different meanings. One of them, the one right on the surface, was a reminder that he would prefer Poppa not be Damon's only influence.

1994

"Okay," Matthew said. "November third." He made a writing gesture, but Cynthia was already taking down the information. "Please tell me you're at least flying him first class. He's going to have little enough time to—okay. Good." He threw a thumbs up to Damon. Cynthia scritched on the cardboard with the marker. "Great. Flight eighty-four out of L.A.X. Got it. Now, wait. Wait. Wait. He tapes on the fourth. Yeah? Okay. Can you just fax me an itinerary, call time and all of that along with the contract?" He closed his eyes and curled his upper lip against his teeth like a Rod Serling impressionist, listening, then said, "Exactly right. That's the number. If I don't find a fax in my hands by—what?—end of day . . .? Terrific! I'll look forward to getting it all and we'll talk more, I'm sure, before—great. Thanks." He pressed the hang up button and turned to Damon.

"Wrong number?" Damon asked.

"You got it."

"For real?" Damon said, but it was only barely a question.

"For real. This is the start of a whole new thing."

Cynthia said, "Damon, this is huge." She hugged him as she handed the cardboard sheet covered in magic marker notes to Matthew.

"You fly out on the third, first class to JFK. You tape on the fourth. You fly home the night of the fourth. You're staying at the Plaza. You're doing four and a half minutes."

"On Letterman," Damon said.

"Oh," Matthew looked worried. "Did you think that was—? No, man. Regis and Kathy Lee."

Knowing this to be a lie, Damon punched Matthew in the arm. "Crap!" He shouted as pain lanced up his forearm from his finger. "I'm putting the splint back on. Jesus."

"Are you okay, Baby?" Cynthia said.

Damon said, "I think I almost blacked out." He squeezed his injured finger in his uninjured grip and felt the throbbing pain as a contrapuntal rhythm against his joyous heartbeat. Despite the extra minute on stage, despite the improvisation at the beginning of the set, he had landed a Letterman spot.

2004

Cynthia hung up the hotel phone, putting the big, old-fashioned plastic receiver on the big, old-fashioned plastic base. The loopy cord hung down beside the little writing desk. She looked at   Damon.

She twinkled. She sparkled. She grinned.

"Wrong number?" Damon said.

"We're pregnant," Cynthia said.

Damon's eyes widened with surprise. Not knowing quite what to say, he heard himself snort in a way that sounded distantly familiar. He searched his feelings and could find no trace of sadness, no spot of anger or fear. He felt a little bit of excited anxiety as though he was just about to go on stage for an important performance, but nothing that could be categorized as a negative emotion anywhere. He said, "Are you sure it's yours?"

Cynthia laughed.

CHAPTER FOURTEEN

2004

D amon and Cynthia stood at the back of the room, his arm around her waist, her hand on his shoulder. They watched the emcee take the stage back from the feature act, their weight a shared thing, hips bumping lightly, playfully.

This time would ordinarily have been spent separately, Cynthia sitting at a table, Damon pacing, building his energy alone at the back. Tonight, though, things were entirely different. They stood together, sharing a small, growing secret. When they looked toward one another, they grinned uncontrollably.

The emcee spoke the words of Damon's introduction, listed his credits, said that he was a funny man and then, the very last thing, his name. The room applauded eagerly and Damon walked onto the stage smiling. He shook the emcee's hand, leaned in to whisper his gratitude into the young man's ear and then moved happily to the microphone.

1994

Back stage, Damon bounced on the balls of his feet, building his energy. He shook out his hands to release tension. He listened to the voice, the voice he knew so well, announcing his credits, his upcoming gigs and then, "making his national television debut . . ." He heard the voice speak his name.

Under the swell of applause he moved onto the flat, waxed floor of the studio. He moved directly to his mark behind the microphone. He waited patiently for the applause to subside so that he could begin his set. For a moment, the first words he was to speak escaped him, creating a moment of absolute silence. Somebody chuckled. Damon looked up at the sound, a bit irritably. That caused someone else to laugh and Damon shifted focus toward that sound. The unspeaking exchange caused a ripple of laughter to pass through the crowd. Damon shrugged. "Maybe I won't tell any jokes tonight," he said. "Just wait 'em out. You'll pop the room." The room laughed and he began his set.

"I love being back on the east coast," he told them. "I grew up in in Ragnarok, New Jersey, the town where Norse Gods go to die. The year after we moved in, their mill closed, so they burned my mother as a witch. This was upsetting to our family as she had nothing to do with the mill closing, and there were so many better reasons." The audience laughed. They laughed at all the right places, though not quite as hard or as loud as Damon was used to hearing them. He wondered if it was a trick of the acoustics or if he was lost in some strange over-focused state, unable to hear properly. His opening run of jokes usually got an applause break when he wrapped it up with Odin, the one-eyed King of the Norse Gods, who could see all of creation, but could not tell how far away any of it was. That day, in Letterman's studio, it got the laugh he usually got   with the introduction of the premise.

The studio was chilly, cold even. Still, he felt sweat trickling down his rib cage, tickling down under his shirt.

Damon was peripherally aware of Mr. Letterman glancing through blue index cards while he did his set.

1983

Damon saw the little red light at the back of the room turn on. The set had been going very well. He'd been riding the wonderful sound of the laughter. He had not yet finished all the jokes he'd planned to do. He had improvised a little bit, a very little bit in the course of the set. He was determined to prove himself a consummate professional by getting off stage the moment he saw the light.

Damon stopped mid-sentence, on his way to a punch line. He said, "Oooh, ladies and gentlemen, the little red light at the back of the room tells me that the producer of tonight's show feels I've run out of wit and charm. I have to go. Thank you all very much," and he was off the stage that fast, that easily.

Moving back up the aisle toward the bar of the Improv, he saw the smiling faces, the audience members grinning at him, giving him thumbs up signals. One young man held a hand up for Damon to high-five as he went past.

The woman who owned the club smiled as he walked past and then followed him out into the bar. "Nice job," she said. She said, "You can start calling in for spots."

That was it. No congratulations. No welcome packet. She turned back to him as she headed back into the show room and added, "Don't talk to the audience about the light. They don't need to know about the light." Then she was gone.

Damon left the club in a dazed state of elation. His ears seemed to buzz with the excitement of it. He found himself out of breath, his heart pounding as though he had run a race while downing amphetamines.

His mind raced ahead through images of a future that would unspool before him now. He was a regular at the Improvisation. He was a professional stand-up comic in New York. Soon he would be on Carson. Then he would sign autographs everywhere he went. He would play Vegas. He would own a penthouse apartment in Manhattan. He would date supermodels. He would deposit checks with a half-dozen zeroes on them before the decimal point. He would buy grass by the ounce instead of the eighth. He would fly first class everywhere and a private helicopter would take him to and from the airport.

Damon Blazer was allowed to call in for spots each week. He was on his way now, and nothing could stop him. Soon, his parents would see the value of what he was doing. Poppa would be so proud of him when he found out.

Realizing that he had failed to find out when he was to call in for spots or how much they paid, Damon considered running back to the club to ask the manager. Instead, he checked his watch, realized the place would still be open when he got home and decided to call in with his questions after he told his parents what had happened.

He realized with a start that he was already inside Grand Central Station. He was standing, pacing actually, at the platform that would soon let him onto the train back to Turdoc, New Jersey. Somehow he had made the long walk across town without really noticing that he was walking at all.

1994

David Letterman walked over to shake Damon's hand and thank him. Then he turned to the camera and threw to commercial.

Damon felt shaken, confused. He felt he should apologize for the set, but he wasn't sure it had been as bad as he thought it had been. Letterman said, "You're pretty funny, kid," and then walked away, back toward his desk.

A young woman in a headset came and took Damon by the elbow. She led him back to the backstage area. As they walked, he felt disconnected from the world around him. "Was that okay?" he asked.

"Yeah," she said, "It was fine. We'll bump up the laughs a little in post." She let go of his arm at the end of the hallway that had the dressing rooms. He moved down the hall, turned into what he thought was his dressing room, found himself face to face for a moment with Elvis Costello. They looked at one another blankly for a moment, neither really having anything to say to the other. Damon said, "Oh. Sorry." And moved on down the hall in search of the proper doorway. He only became certain of which one it was when Matthew emerged and came toward him.

"That was brilliant, Damon."

"Really?"

"'Maybe I won't tell any jokes tonight.'" He quoted. "Fucking hilarious."

"Okay," Damon said. "Good." He was not entirely convinced. He said, "The girl told me they would bump up the laughs before it airs."

"Good," Matthew said. "Excellent!"

Damon felt a little bit nauseated.

2004

Damon came off stage. He heard the roaring applause of the Bahia Resort's audience and saw only Cynthia's beaming face as she moved toward him and took him in her arms.

"Are you kidding me?" she asked. Damon had no idea what she was talking about.

"Um . . ." he said.

"If I'd known pregnancy was going to make you that funny, I'd've gotten knocked up a long time ago."

"Really? It was good?" Damon searched his memory, tried to get his bearings, but he found he could remember nothing at all about the set he'd just performed. Moments of his personal history shifted and melted in his mind, a set at the Improv, the train ride home afterward, his first Letterman appearance, but he couldn't seem to remember a moment of the performance he'd just given seconds earlier.

"What was there--?" she asked. "Like twenty minutes of brand new stuff tonight? Plus the new tags, the new callbacks. You were on fire."

Damon felt a slight twinge of panic and then began to recover his stride. Pieces of the show came back to him. He had talked about the pregnancy. He had gotten laughs. He would have to ask the club owner if there was a tape of the show. If not, he would sit with Cynthia and they would reconstruct it as best they could from memory. He had been lost in the roar and rush of the crowd. He had been consumed by the energy of the room and driven by the knowledge that he was about to be a father, that Cynthia would be a mother, drawn by a future that was suddenly taking on new shape, clearer purpose.

"I was . . . this was a good show, wasn't it?"

"Damon," Cynthia said very seriously, "If your grandfather were alive today, he would've called it your bar mitzvah."

Hearing that, Damon choked, then coughed to cover the reaction. He knew what Cynthia meant and, more importantly, he knew that Cynthia knew how his mind worked, knew his history and his thoughts, knew his memories and his references.

As Cynthia kissed him, he heard the continuing applause of the crowd, still cheering his performance as the emcee cleared his throat into the microphone time and again, striving to regain control of the room.

1982

Damon sat beside the hospital bed feeling the hard plastic of the chair's arm, scratching at the fake-leather-textured surface with a thumbnail. "Can

I ask you something, Poppa?"

"You know you can."

Damon shrugged. "Sometimes I'm afraid you'll get mad at me. That I'll ask you something you think I should already know."

"You're this worried about my sensitivities? Really, Kid?"

"I guess. Yeah."

"How much can you upset me after giving me Alzheimer's to make people laugh?"

"Sorry about that. I won't do the joke anymore if. . ."

"It got a laugh. We both know you'll do it again at some point. You might as well do it with my blessing. It's fine, Damon. What do you want to ask?"

"Do you think I'm ready to get a showcase at the Improv? At Catch a Rising Star? At the real clubs?"

"Sure."

"I mean, I've been doing pretty well at Mickey Tam's every week for a couple of months now."

"I'm sure you have."

"And I'm writing material pretty steadily. I've got a solid fifteen. Maybe twenty."

"You can stop selling me, Kid. Go ahead and showcase."

"What if I blow it, though? What if—"

"Kid, you showcase. It goes great and you get in or it goes bad and you showcase again. It's a fucking nightclub in New York. It's not your whole career. You got hundreds of shows ahead of you. Thousands. Go ahead. Give it a shot."

Damon tried to breathe in the idea of thousands of shows ahead of him. He tried to imagine the scope of time that made a career. He said, "You really think

I should?"

"Yeah. I do. You're a funny boy, Damon."

Damon winced. A year out of high school, twenty minutes of good jokes ready to go, he felt stung. He said, "I'm a man, Poppa."

"You're not that funny," Poppa said.

2004

Damon and Cynthia stood in the night air on the little wooden bridge over the seal pond. Asleep, the seals looked like great, gray shadows. Great, gray, snorting shadows.

"The seal joke got a great laugh," Cynthia told him. "You can't do it anywhere but here, but it got a great laugh."

"I did a seal joke?"

"Unbelievable," Cynthia said. "Yeah. Yeah, you did. You said you loved the seals here. This afternoon you stood there just watching them and after two hours or so, it was so cute, one of them woke up and rolled over."

Damon chuckled. "That is funny," he said.

"Yeah."

They stood together. They breathed the salt air. They thought about a baby, about pregnancy, about the future.

Cynthia said, "You know things are going to change, right?"

Damon nodded, but he was not thinking of the same things she was.

Cynthia said, "I can't be a placeholder anymore."

"What?" Damon said.

"In your act it's fine. 'My girlfriend,' gives people the information they need to get to the punch line. But we're about to have a kid, Damon. I can't just be the girlfriend anymore."

"Are you saying you want to get married?"

"No. I mean . . . if you're proposing, I'll say yes. In a heartbeat. But no. That's not what I'm saying. Girlfriend, wife, whatever. The point is, sometimes I think—sometimes it feels as though we're all extras. You know? The people in movies who walk by on the sidewalk in the New York scenes but don't really have a story of their own. Me, your mom, your brother . . . even Poppa when you talk about him. Now there's going to be this other person we're responsible for. Both of us. I need to know that I have a partner in that. I need to know that I *am* a partner in that. Do you understand what I'm saying?"

Damon nodded. He felt shame and guilt. He hated himself for how well he knew what she was saying. He hated himself even more because now, for the first time, he felt pangs of fear over the pregnancy. The thought of a baby hadn't scared him. The thought of parenthood hadn't worried him in the least. No. The only thing that had brought fear into his heart was the thought of being a little bit less self-involved. He didn't know whether he was capable.

"You understand that I'm still a comic, right?"

Cynthia laughed. She squeezed him tight against her. "I do."

"Okay," Damon said.

CHAPTER FIFTEEN

2004

Damon drove. Cynthia slept beside him in the passenger's seat. Her chest rose and fell with each breath. He watched the road, but he listened to her breathe. He tried hard to allow her presence in the car to have its own place, to imagine what she might be dreaming about as he steered.

Bits of his performances drifted through his thoughts, jokes he had created on the spot that he might be able to use again surfaced for him to examine and rework.

He tried to put himself on the outside, standing with Cynthia near the kitchen door at the back of the club room, watching. He realized that she probably did not stand there through the show, that she had probably found a seat if there was one available after he was done pacing and safely on stage, and then came back there to meet him when he came off. He imagined her sitting back there in the dark and tried to imagine himself watching from there, from a back table.

1992

Damon watched his father turn the glass of scotch on the paper cocktail napkin. The damp edges at the bottom of the glass softened the paper and now the napkin tore like dough beneath a cookie cutter. When his father took a sip, the rough-edged circle of paper stuck to the bottom of the glass leaving a round stencil on the table.

"The weird thing," Damon said, "is that no matter how many people tell me I'm funny, no matter how well a show goes, the next day I'm still asking Matt if it went okay, fishing for compliments. It's like . . . I don't know. It's like I can never get enough reassurance that I didn't imagine it as being better than it really was."

Dad snorted. It was a snort that said, "Does this really surprise you?" and also, "This is why comedy is a lesser form than literature or theater," and also, "I'm not sure if you really want to hear my thoughts on this."

Damon heard all of these things in the snort and still he said, "What does that mean?"

"What does what mean?" His father asked.

"The little snort. What did that mean?"

Dad gave a shrug that suggested he was about to say something profound and a little bit dangerous. He had already decided to say it and now he was just going to have to face the repercussions if any should come. He took an extra moment, watching travelers hurry past to their boarding gates or their Cinnabon purchases before he said, "When you perform as a comic, you are the object of the experience, rather than the subject of the experience. Even as an actor, it's true to some degree, but at least there, you're working within this framework in which you submerge yourself into the subjective experience of the character. As a comic you stand there in front of   an audience and expose yourself and they judge you for—what?–twenty minutes? Forty-five minutes? You are the thing on display. A room full of people thinks it's gotten to know you. A lot of those people are confused into thinking you've gotten to know them. But the only you that's there is the one that's being projected on to you. Afterward, you need someone to tell you who you were during that time. You want your identity back and the only way you can imagine getting it back is to hear that you were funny. Comedy is dangerous, Damon." Simon sighed. He moved an ice cube around in the scotch with his fingertip, feeling the way it melted against his warmth. He said, "I don't know if you have any idea how much I worry about you."

Damon did not bother to hear the last sentence at all. He was far too wrapped up in other things his father had said.

"Huh. That's why after the show they want to talk to me. They all think we're friends."

"How's that work out for you?"

Damon shook his head. "I start having these conversations and they always turn a little bit weird. It all starts out okay and then they turn out to be . . . sort of stupid. Or just boring. And they always want to tell me a joke."

Simon Blazer snorted.

1984

Damon held the microphone as Poppa had told him, lightly between his thumb and middle finger. He moved the stand back and to the side, out of his way without tangling it in the cord. He brought the stand back, put the microphone back into the cradle, took up the mic and moved the stand away again.

"Now listen," Poppa said. Damon listened. He always did when Poppa spoke. "It doesn't matter whether you're performing to two thousand people at ten o'clock at night or to ten people at two in the morning, there's a crazy thing that happens. They think they were as much a part of the show as you were. They can't help it. They're civilians. They can't get their heads around what the hell is going on. You keep doing the jokes. They keep laughing. They think you're working together on it or something. Never mind that it's completely crazy. It's what they think. You get me?"

"Um," Damon said.

"How do I say this? All right." He crinkled up his aging brow, searching for words to explain a complex thought. He was not a man who intellectualized comfortably or regularly. He was not a man who got bogged down in the thinking. He was a one-liner sort of guy, a fast banter sort of guy. He said, "They're all sitting out here doing one thing, and you're up there, the only one in the room doing something entirely different. Well, you and the waitresses. They got a whole other thing going on."

"How do you make a comic's dick hard?" Damon asked.

"How do you make a comic's dick hard?" Poppa obliged automatically.

"Put on an apron and carry a tray."

"Nice," Poppa said. He went on as though there had been no interruption, but there had and it had

been exactly the right interruption. It had put him at
ease again. It had put him back on his rhythm. "At
the end of the show, the civilians think they've
shared something with you. A– what?–a moment. A .
. . thing. You understand? They don't realize that
they shared something together and you were the only one who wasn't part of it. They're out drinking,
laughing, having a great time, maybe getting laid,
whatever. You're the only one in the room working,
doing your job. As far as they're concerned, your
whole job is to have a great time partying at a night
club. They don't know you're sweating your *toches*
off, making a living, keeping track of time, the feeling
in the room, the pace of the show, getting them laid,
making their night fun for them. They think you're
part of the crowd. And you don't ever tell 'em otherwise. Not ever. They want to buy you a drink after
the show, you have a drink with them after the show.
They want to introduce you to their girl, their mom,
whatever, you shake the hands, thank *them* for the
great show. Even the hecklers. Fucking hecklers. I
hate 'em. But you gotta be nice to 'em. They're your
biggest fans, if it goes right. They think they were
part_ of the show. They don't even know they're civilians. They think they're straight men. They think
they helped you up there. You let 'em think that. The
club doesn't have someone to shut 'em up or haul
'em out, you never let on to the heckler that you wish
they did. You thank 'em up and down. 'Thanks for
playing. Thanks for being a good sport.' Never mind
they screwed up your timing, stepped on your jokes,
fucked up your set. It's not your job to give audience
lessons. You understand? You're an entertainer."

The urgency with which Poppa delivered his   advice now was apparent. It seemed to rush from him in a torrent of words, an accelerating download of Alvie Grunman's lifetime of experience. Damon took in the advice, seeing it as useful to his craft, important to his career. He did not notice the near panic in his grandfather's voice, the desperate need to pass his knowledge on, to know that it would not go with him to his grave.

Damon did not have time, in his twentieth year on the planet, to think about what hecklers Poppa had encountered and thanked. He did not have room in his psyche to take in the depth and the breadth of experience the old man sought to impart. He had the narrow focus of a young man at the start of his career and he took in the information as if it had been mined from the hard rock of time just for his benefit. He could not recognize the vast mountain of experience from which the nuggets were now sluiced by Poppa's flowing words. He could only gather up the sparkling bits of wisdom as they were tossed at him, collecting them, striving not to let a single one slip from his hurried grasp.

1992

"Poppa told me I always have to be good to them," Damon said. "He said it's important not to remind them that they're civilians. He said it's my responsibility as an entertainer."

"Entertainer," Dad said derisively.

"What's wrong with that?"

"Entertainment," Simon said, sliding into his

most academic persona, "is the word people use when they don't want to take responsibility for what they're saying with their art." He let those words hang there for a moment. Then he said, "That's good. There's a whole article in that. An essay or a lecture." Damon snorted and realized how much he sounded like his father. He snorted because there were so many things he wanted to say, so many things he wanted not to say because they were funny and his father wouldn't be willing to hear the humor, wouldn't be willing to laugh. Hearing that snort come from his own nose, he suddenly understood how many things his father had left unsaid in his lifetime. He understood how often his father silenced his own true voice for fear of sounding cruel or angry or unfair. In that moment, Damon saw his father as a sad figure, a tragic figure. He knew for the very first time that Simon Blazer was a man who snorted because he could not write a joke.

"There was a time," Dad went on, "that comics were part of the national artscape. It really looked as though comedy and songwriting were going to take their proper place among the arts, that they could help to shape the culture and the society the same way painting did in the renaissance, the way filmmaking did in Europe with Buñuel and Renoir and Truffaut. You had Lord Buckley and Lenny Bruce picking away at the bourgeois sensibility of the fifties and the early sixties, Carlin unraveling the repression of the middle class in the seventies. Then . . . I don't know what happened. It was as if all these guys started going on stage imitating one another, doing the same rhythms, the same jokes, the same ideas." His eyes danced. He seemed to be reading a dense page of script that hung before him in the air as he explored thoughts on comedy the way he examined dramatic structure or literature, preparing to present it to a classroom full of college students, wanting not only to share his insight, but also to prove his ability to see more deeply into the material than those around him. This was Simon's great joy, digging down through art, through culture, through trends in the collective experience to find the underpinnings. Whatever his personal reactions were to a thing, be it the world of comedy or a single curve in a complex sculpture, he was quite certain that if he could just express the underlying, hidden message of the thing, he could prove his opinion correct.

"The boom," Damon said.

"What?" Dad asked. For a moment it was as if he had entirely forgotten that his son was sitting with him in the airport, that he was not alone, ordering thoughts silently in his own head.

1978

Damon rode in the back seat of the 1974 Town and Country station wagon. The music of John Williams pounded majestically in his head. X-wing fighters darted across an imagined skyscape.

"It's the same problem," Simon said to Alice in the front seat, "that I have with all war movies. It's the same problem, come to think of it, that I have with war in general."

1977

"Did that change the way you saw the whole world, when Trixie made you laugh?"

Poppa chuckled. "Sort of. Yeah. Not . . . that's not what I was talking about before, though."

"I know," Damon said.

"Do you?"

Damon broke off a chunk of bread for the ducks, but he did not toss it at the water. He held it between his thumb and forefinger and he rolled it into a ball. He wasn't sure if he did know what his grandfather had been talking about. He also wasn't sure that he didn't. He couldn't quite remember how far into it Poppa had gone. The only thing he knew with absolute certainty was that he loved listening to his grandfather talk. He loved hearing everything his Grandfather had to say. He said nothing and waited.

"Some comedy . . . let's say one of these new guys, George Carlin, one of those guys, these guys who do observations that don't look like regular jokes. You know what I'm talking about?"

"Uh-huh," Damon knew exactly what he was talking about. He didn't really think of George Carlin as a 'new guy' but he'd listened very closely to all of Carlin's records. He knew all about the jokes that don't look like jokes.

"He might start off with something totally innocuous. He'll say, you know, I don't know . . . he'll say, 'Supermarkets are bizarre.' Right?"

"Okay . . ." Damon said. He couldn't actually imagine George Carlin saying that, but he knew this was going somewhere. He didn't want to break Poppa's flow.

"Now, you hear that—anybody hears that, the first thought is, 'No they're not. I go in a supermarket every week.' But then he backs it up he says . . . crap. I shoulda had one in mind. What's something you see in a supermarket every week?"

Damon said, "I don't know. TV dinners. Frozen pizza?"

"Oh. Good. Okay. So he says, 'I saw a frozen pizza. It said on the box, "Serving suggestion: keep frozen." People buy these things every week. How many of them you think try out the suggestion?'"

Damon chuckled.

"Okay," Alvie Grunman conceded, wincing slightly to dismiss the shame of a comic who has allowed an imperfect joke to be told. "Not the best I ever wrote. But still, let's say you saw that on a pizza box and you wrote the joke . . ."

"Shouldn't it be, I don't know, 'Food packaging is bizarre?'" Damon asked.

"Probably. Yeah. That's not the point. I say supermarkets are bizarre and then I do a joke—and let's pretend it's a good joke—about something you see in the supermarket every week. Now, every time you go into the supermarket, every time you see that thing, you think, 'Wow. That really *is* bizarre.' Yeah? You with me so far?"

Damon shrugged. He nodded. 'So far' told him there was more yet to come.

"Good. Now you've changed the way people see supermarkets forever. Or frozen pizza. Or packaging or whatever. But let's say you're talking about something else. Let's say–okay–here's one from a friend of mine a few years ago. He did a thing on the Smothers Brothers, brilliant sketch the censors cut outta the show. It's a general talking to a private and he says, 'Get out there! Do it for your country!' and the private says, 'My country isn't out there! That's someone else's country out there!' The General says, 'Hey, there are powerful people in Washington who think this is worth killing for and they've spent a lot of time and energy convincing you that it's worth dying for!' You know why the censors wouldn't put that on television?"

"'Cause they were a bunch of conservative pricks?"

"No. Well, yes. But no. It was because it got a huge laugh in rehearsal. And that made it dangerous. If you can make a supermarket look bizarre, think about what you can do to a war."

"M*A*S*H," Damon said.

"Exactly," Poppa told him.

1978

Damon knew the tone of voice, even if he was not certain of the specific issue his father had with this movie. Simon hadn't liked the film and he was about to expound upon the reasons that he didn't like it. He had a problem with the message or the politics. He felt the characters were two dimensional or the dialogue didn't ring true. It was sentimental (always an insult when used by Simon Blazer) or dishonest or campy, a word Damon had heard many times and still hadn't quite been able to figure out from context. He couldn't figure out what a word could possibly mean that had been used to describe both *Batman and Robin* on television and the Gene Kelly musical, *An American in Paris*.

"I know, Honey," Alice said. Damon's mother knew that Damon had enjoyed the movie. She was a little bit torn. On the one hand, she didn't want the pleasure of a good time at the movies to be taken from him. On the other hand, she knew exactly where Simon was going with his thought and she certainly thought it was a valid line of reasoning for Damon to be exposed to.

"In order for the antagonists to go around killing people and remain heroes in their own minds, and in the minds of the audience or . . . the public . . . you have to create a dehumanized enemy. And boy do they find an easy way to do that in this movie. Huh? Put 'em all in identical plastic uniforms, so they don't even have features and then there's no problem having your good guys slaughter them. You never have to think that there are people in those suits being blown up and burned and cast out into space and what-have-you."

"It was essentially a re-examination of the Arthurian Legend," Alice said.

"Sure," Simon said. "And every Western ever made with the bad guy savage Indians. And all that god-awful World War Two stuff with the Yellow Horde and the Jerries coming over the fucking ridge."

Damon pressed an imaginary switch that turned on his light saber. He said, "Mrrrrr-mmmmm-rrrrrrrmmmmmmmm."

"How you doing back there, Kiddo?" Simon asked.

1992

"The comedy boom," Damon said. "It can't last much longer. It's been going on for about ten years."

"What do you mean?" Simon asked. He seemed a little bit startled to hear his son bring up something that was surely an important, widespread cultural event of which he had somehow remained entirely unaware. He sipped his airport scotch to hide his confusion.

"It really started before I got into the business with the movie FAME in 1980 where the kid goes out on stage for his first time at Catch a Rising Star and does great and suddenly he's a working comic in NY. Then in '88 PUNCHLINE made it worse with all that crap about how you have to get on stage and throw away your act and just improvise to be funny. But the thing is, all of the people who grew up watching Carlin and the Smothers Brothers and Flip Wilson suddenly thought they understood how to be comics 'cause they'd seen it in the movies. Plus, there were all the new cable channels doing showcase stuff so there was a lot more airtime available if you could just come up with a good, tight six minutes. *Comedy on the Road, Evening at the Improv, Comedy Express, Comic Strip Live, Short Attention Span Theater.* There were dozens of these things. So it looked like a gold mine to some people who had never even really thought about comedy before. Workshops opened up and comedy classes. Every bar that couldn't get people in to dance after the disco craze took down the mirror ball and started up a comedy night, so there are all these one-nighters everywhere you can do. When the market is that wide, there's bound to be a glut of mediocre product. You know?"

Dad snorted. It was a sad, hurt, pained, slightly worried snort. "Product?" He said. "Is that really how you think about your craft?"

Damon felt very, very small suddenly. And very young.

2004

Damon felt very, very grown up as he followed the 405 back up toward Los Angeles. He reached out to rest his hand on Cynthia's thigh as he drove and he noticed that he was smiling just a little bit. He said, "You know what, Honey?"

In her sleep, Cynthia said, "Mrrrm?"

He said, "I have to start thinking a lot more about what I'm saying on stage."

CHAPTER SIXTEEN

2004

After the long drive and the hot shower, it felt good to be at home in their own bed. Damon wondered what could possibly be taking s l e e p so long to come. He listened to the sounds of the night, the tapping of the eucalyptus tree against the window. He watched the movement of shadows against the wall.

Warm under the blankets, he moved a foot free of the covering to help regulate his body temperature. M. Furry Abraham offered a warning sound, somewhere between a purr and a growl. Damon pulled his foot back into the overheated safety under the blanket. M. Furry Abraham had very strict rules about feet outside the blankets and he only gave one warning before enforcing the regulations with sharp claws.

The familiar weight of Cynthia in the bed beside him felt safe and comforting, even as the thought of the baby she was manufacturing grew slowly more terrifying with each incremental cellular generation.

He held his hand up in front of the window, examining its shape as a black shadow against the dim night sky of the city. He folded it into a bunny shape, curled his fingers so that it looked like the paw of a huge dog, made a silhouette vaguely reminiscent of Kermit the Frog. He imagined learning to make complex shadow puppets to entertain a child. He imagined a child.

He let his knuckles brush gently against Cynthia's arm. She stirred a bit in her sleep, rolling clos- er to him. He turned to look at her sweet face, wrinkles from the pillowcase molded into her cheek. He raised himself up on one elbow and kissed her on the oddly sculptured cheek. He kissed her jawline. He kissed her ear.

She awoke, startled and said, "Ahh! What the hell!?!"

Damon started back at the unexpected exclamation. "Sorry, I was–"

"Jesus, Damon," she said. "You scared the crap out of me."

"I was kissing you."

"I was sleeping."

"Yeah."

1994

After sleeping on the plane, Damon was fairly free of Vicodin. His finger hurt. He was still a little bit flushed with adrenalin, pissed off and tired. Damon didn't want to be that guy anymore. He didn't want to be the guy that whined about how unfair it was that his brother bullied him, who flinched when his brother came near him, who held his tongue rather than risking another beating.

"You know what?" he said. "Pull over."

"What are you talking about?"

"I'm talking about you pulling the fuck over."

"What? You gonna walk back to the house from here? It's like five miles," Lenny said.

"No. Pull over and get out of the car. I'm gonna kick your ass."

"You're not gonna kick my ass, Damon."

"How can you be so sure? Maybe I am."

"Really? 'Cause I'm pretty sure the closest you've ever come to fighting was lying on the ground getting pummeled and also you have a broken finger or some shit. So, seriously, how are you gonna kick my ass?"

"Pull the car over and find out, you prick. I don't want to do this in front of Mom on the day I get back into town and I don't want to sit around the house pretending I'm not pissed off as hell. You want to prove how tough you are? You think it's so funny to make me flinch? Pull over and see how funny it is when I'm pounding your face in."

Lenny snorted a derisive sort of snort. It sounded only vaguely like Dad, but it was close enough to push Damon's buttons. He drove his left hand across Lenny's face in a punch that a man can only throw when he's sitting in a passenger's seat and striking out at someone whose focus is entirely on the road. It was a slow, sloppy punch that landed squarely on the hinge of the jaw and yet had almost no effect whatsoever.

Lenny turned to look at Damon in disbelief. In so doing, he swerved momentarily into the opposite lane. A car, still a decent distance up the road, blared its horn. Lenny steered back to the right, but he overcompensated just a bit and the car spun a hundred and eighty degrees, coming to a complete stop on the shoulder of the road facing back the way they'd come.

His own adrenalin pumping, Lenny jumped out of the car and pounded on the roof of the vehicle as Damon wrestled with his seat belt and the door handle, his efforts hampered by the splinted finger.

"What the fuck is wrong with you?" Lenny shouted at him.

"Me? I'm not the one driving into oncoming traffic, skidding across the road, Lenny. I'm not the one who refused to pull over when I told you to."

"I'm driving, you moron. You don't hit a guy when he's driving."

"No? When do you hit a guy, Len? It seems to be your field of expertise. Maybe your only field of expertise. Why don't you enlighten me? When do you hit a guy?"

"I don't need this shit. Get in the car," Lenny said.

"Now you're afraid to fight me? I finally throw one punch and suddenly you don't want to play anymore is that it? You coward."

"Damon, you're seriously freaking out, here. Just calm down. Is this 'cause Dad is dead?"

"What? No. This is . . . maybe. You know what? Maybe it is. Maybe now that Dad is dead I finally have to stand up for myself. Maybe . . . I don't know. Maybe I broke my finger 'cause I thought if I was injured you'd treat me differently or I wouldn't have to worry about having you come at me or whatever. I don't know. But you know what I do know?"

"You know that you've turned into a raving lunatic?"

Damon launched himself at his older brother, lost in a stupefying rage. With full commitment, the momentum of his attack and a lifetime of fury behind it, he threw what was intended as a haymaker of a wild punch. He realized in the split second before the blow landed that the splint had kept him from bending his index finger. He attacked his brother with a full-force poke to the chest.

Pain lanced up his arm, across his shoulders and seemed to explode, white and black and white again across his brain. He noticed shapes in the pain as if he were staring at clouds. He wondered, in a confused, distant way, what that humming noise was.

1982

Poppa examined the creases in the back of his hand left by the oxygen tube that he'd been sleeping on. He thought that those creases made him look sicklier than the tubes across his nose, the drip running into his vein, the hospital gown, the pale skin. Those just made him look old. The impression of the tube on his arm made him look like wormwood, like he was being eaten away. It made him look frail.

He had been thinking about this for a long time, had been working out in his mind how he was going to say it, what his reasoning was. Now that it was time, he wanted to make sure he got it just right. If Damon was going to do this thing, he had to understand why he was doing it. He had to understand how important it was. He had to be doing it for the right reasons, not just because he had promised.

"When a person dies, Damon, it screws things up

for everyone. Not just, you know, 'Oh, we're sad. So-and-so is gone.' I mean, there's the funeral, there's wills to be read and arguments over the—whatever—the recliner and what gets thrown out and what gets kept. There's all sorts of arguments and people angry at one another for what they said once a long time ago or what they forgot to say yesterday. It's a big thing when somebody dies. Plus, you know, all the questions. Heaven and hell and reincarnation."

"You believe in life after death, Poppa?" Damon asked.

"Me? Yeah. But, you know, mostly the life of other people. Not the dead guy so much."

Damon chuckled.

"Now shut up. I'm explaining something to you."

"Sorry," Damon said. He clutched the brown paper bag, uncertain he could bring himself to do what Poppa wanted. He still wasn't even certain it was what the old man would really want. It was a funny idea, a funny thought, but in reality it seemed so wrong.

"Now, there's never been a person died that someone didn't say at some point, 'Someday we'll look back on this and laugh.' During the reading of the will, when someone's sniffling over how touched they are by what's been left for 'em or in the car to the cemetery, when the wife is wailing like a ban-shee. When Trixie died—shame you never got to meet Trixie. God she was funny—I was a mess. Losing weight, sitting in a little apartment on Avenue B. I couldn't stop drinking about that woman." His eyes stung a bit just thinking about her, thinking about that apartment without her in it. The smell of her hung in that apartment until the day he moved out.

"That's funny."

"Thanks."

"You know, in a country music sort of way."

"Fuck you, you little prick," Poppa said. "Anyway, even then, people kept saying, 'Someday you're gonna look back on this and laugh.' That's a load of crap. Saddest time of my life. I don't look back on it and laugh. I look back on that and if I'm shaving, I cut myself a little bit. Things I should've said to her before she was gone. She knew. You know? But still. I should've said."

Damon wasn't sure what Poppa was talking about, but he had never seen his grandfather look so sad, so old, so weak.

"My point is, the times you look back at and laugh are the times you laughed, not the other times. The times you talk about over and over again are the time Aunt Matilda fell out of her chair onto the lemon meringue pie or whatever. Not the time she fell on the ice and broke her hip. When I'm gone, I want people to have those memories. People want to forget the sad times. The laughter they want to review every chance they get, every time they get together, they tell the funny stories. Laughs last, Damon. Only the laughs. I want them to say, 'You remember Alvie Grunman?' and then start to laugh. I don't want 'em to get all weepy."

Damon held up the brown paper bag. "You think this'll do that?"

"Are you kidding me, Damon? That's gonna do it like nobody's business."

"Mom'll never forgive me, Poppa."

"No. Your Mom knows more than you think. She grew up with me, you know."

Damon nodded slowly.

"Your father. He's the one who'll never forgive you. And your brother. Oy."

1994

Clouds shifted and melted in a flashing, end-of-a-movie-reel sort of way. Their light show was accompanied by a humming, but it was a strange humming. Damon seemed able to hear the vibration of the sound, the individual sine waves that made up the tone. He focused on it with an intense curiosity, slowing it in his ears until it became a throbbing note. It thudded in time with the flashing of the clouds. He watched the flashing, pulsing clouds as he swam up through the deep water toward them. The water was cold against his hand, against his finger, against . . .

He twitched and realized he was twitching. He wondered if he had been twitching for a long time, if that was the sensation that had seemed to be a tone, a throbbing. Then he recognized the throbbing as occurring in his finger, a low pulsing ache that matched his heart- beat. He thought that perhaps the tone he had heard moments earlier had been an interpretation of his racing heart, now slowing to a more normal rate again. That thought melted away as he realized that the sound he had heard as a piercing tone was, in fact, his older brother's hysterical laughter.

"What the hell happened?" Damon asked, staggering to his feet.

"I'm sorry I'm laughing," Lenny said, and he genuinely was sorry. "Are you okay? God. That was the funniest thing I've ever seen."

Damon blinked slowly. "I passed out, didn't I?"

"Yeah. Yeah, you did. I'm gonna have a bruise!" Lenny laughed, rubbing the spot on his chest where Damon had poked him with his splinted finger.

2004

"I really wasn't trying to startle you," Damon said.

"I know. I know. Just . . . wow. Give me a sec. My heart is racing."

"Mine too," Damon said. He wiggled an eyebrow at her.

The smell of his body reached her nostrils. It had never bothered her before, but now, with the hormones rearranging themselves in her system, his musk was heavy, dense. It seemed to suffocate her. A wave of uncomfortable dizziness swept through her.

"Damon," she said, "I really don't want you to take this the wrong way."

"Okay," he said. There was a nervous hesitation in his voice.

"I think I'm going to throw up."

Cynthia threw aside the blankets and raced to the bathroom. Damon heard the wrenching sounds of her ordeal as he lay back in bed.

"Wow," M. Furry Abraham commented.

"Yeah," Damon agreed.

CHAPTER SEVENTEEN

2004

Damon sat on the floor. He pressed his back to the bathroom door. He listened to the sound of Cynthia's retching. He wondered if there was something he should be saying, some sort of comfort he could offer through the closed door that would soothe her.

"Do you want me to come in and hold your hair?" he asked.

"No," she said. After a long pause she added, "Thank you."

M. Furry Abraham curled into his lap. Damon absently scratched a small circle just below the cat's ear.

"M. Furry Abraham is worried about you."

"Tell him I'm fine."

"She says she's fine."

M. Furry Abraham sighed the sigh of the tolerant cat, the wise cat who puts up with his housemate's absurd antics and anthropomorphisations primarily because of their opposable-thumbed ability to work a can opener.

"He says we're both idiots," Damon told Cynthia.

"He's half right," she said through the closed door.

"Very nice," Damon said.

1985

Damon carefully removed the markings from his floor boards. He had liked the idea of building the little sundial, but now it just felt like a reminder of the passage of time. Damon did not want to think about the passage of time.

Since Poppa's funeral, he had been smoking a lot more pot. He had been sleeping later and later into the day. He had been staying awake later and later into the night. He sat alone in his gloom and sucked down giant bong hits while the television showed him infomercials about party lines that he could call to meet hot women in his neighborhood.

He thought about the skinny women who sat outside in his neighborhood with their missing teeth and their visible bruises. He had the sense that there was a bit to be written about the party lines and the junkies outside his apartment, but he couldn't quite put the pieces together. It all seemed too sad to be funny.

He used a thumbnail to work a bit of masking-tape adhesive from a floorboard. He went to his desk to fill a bong hit and noticed the red light flashing on his answering machine. He couldn't imagine when he had missed a call. When he'd been in the shower early that afternoon? When he walked down to the candy store to buy an eighth of an ounce? Had the light been flashing unnoticed since yesterday when he went to buy coffee? He pressed the button with the forward-pointing triangle and listened to his message.

"Hi, Damon," said a voice that sounded vaguely familiar. "This is Andy Lebaron at the Friars' Club. I don't know if you know who I am, but—" Damon knew exactly who Andy Lebaron was. What he didn't know was why on earth a ninety-year-old ventriloquist would be calling him from the Friars' Club.

1982

Damon sat down in the waiting room, clutching the brown paper bag. He thought about putting it in the trash bin, just pushing the bag through the spring-hinged lid and letting the whole idea go. It's not as if Poppa would know the difference. Does a promise matter if the person it's made to is already dead? It wasn't as if this was in his will, a legal obligation of some sort. He could just put the bag in the trash and never think about it again.

He rested his elbows on his knees, sitting in the hard-backed plastic chair and gripped the crumpled mouth of the bag in his sweating hand. It seemed the sort of decision that would be easy to make. It seemed to him that this was the sort of thing that should just be done with already. He wasn't sure that his love for his grandfather outweighed his commitment to the social contract. He knew that it was the disruption of etiquette that made the idea worthwhile. If not for that, Poppa would never have thought of it, would never have seen its value, would never have made him promise.

In other seats around him, people worried about

loved ones. People leafed absently through obsolete magazines trying to distract themselves from the tragedies into which their lives were descending or into which they feared their lives might be about to descend.

Damon could feel their concerns. He could see in their eyes and their twitchy sips of consciousness-sustaining vending-machine coffee that they feared the worst. They worried about their finances, their loved ones, the changes that might be bearing down on them due to an auto accident, an illness, a mis-step on a wet floor. He wondered how, surrounded by such people, he could be so utterly stopped, so deep-ly affected by a joke, and a prop joke at that.

1977

Poppa made his duck noise and watched the ducks turn their heads toward him. "You know why they look at me like that?" He asked.

"Why?" Damon asked.

"'Cause of my accent."

Damon laughed.

"What you just did there, that's how I know you can be funny."

"'Cause I laughed at your duck joke?"

"No, Damon. Not that. Before that. 'Cause you were my straight man. Just for a second, but exactly right."

"What?" Damon asked.

"I said, 'You know why they look at me like that?' and then I gave you time to answer. People who   get it, who get how jokes work, the rhythm and the timing, they know what to say next. You say, 'Why?' or 'Why do they look at you like that?' That's the thing I need for the punch line. That's the key to straight man. Take the gecko joke. How's that work with a straight man?"

Damon blinked for a moment, playing the joke as dialogue and his eyes went wide. Poppa wiggled his eyebrows, seeing the young man put it together in his mind.

"Oh!" Damon said, excited. "What did one iguana say to the other iguana?"

Poppa said, "What did one iguana say to the other iguana?"

"Hey! Is there a gecko in here?"

The ducks seemed to laugh at the little routine.

"It's way better that way," Damon said.

"Yeah," Poppa said.

"Funnier. Shorter. You know? Less words," Damon said.

"It's piss fucking elegant, Damon. That's what it is when you add the straight man, Damon."

"Yeah," Damon said.

"But if I were a civilian I'd be just as likely to say, 'I don't know. What?' or, you know, 'I have no idea.'"

"Or if you were my brother, Lenny, you'd say, 'That's fuckin' stupid. Iguana's can't talk, you stupid fuck.'"

Poppa laughed.

"Thanks for being a straight man for me, Poppa. That's nice."

"Only for people I love, Damon. Only for people I love."

Alvie Grunman looked out at the pond. Damon

imagined that when he talked to his cat and his duck, he was willing to be a straight man for them. He didn't imagine the cat and the duck saying anything funny, though.

1974

Damon moved the syrup around on his plate.

"But when people go to hear a comic aren't   they all thinking, 'Let's see if he can make us laugh?'" Damon said.

"Yes. And they want him to be able to. But even so, it's the guy's job to make them forget that. You know why you hear hack comics say, 'But seriously, folks,' all the time?"

"Why?"

"'Cause they can't think of a better way to confuse the audience into coming with them on the next premise."

Damon nodded slowly, thinking that through.

"The only way a joke works, kid, is if the   people listening forget to be listening for the joke for a second. You wanna do that to a room full of people every couple of seconds for an hour, you gotta be pretty damn clever about it. There was a joke I used to do, what? Ten years ago. After Trixie died. I was not a happy man. I was old enough already I could play grumpy old Jew. You know? You were a baby, Lenny was still real little, but I used to say, 'My daughter is all excited. She said she's gonna send her kid to summer camp. He's gonna ride horses. Play guitar. I told her, *I went to a camp once.*'"

"I don't get it," Damon said.

"That's not funny, Alvie," Simon told him.

"Bullshit. Big laughs. And not just shock laughs, either. The good, think-about-it-for-a-second-and-then-put-a-martini-through-your-nose laughs."

"Really, Dad? You were doing holocaust jokes?" Alice said in disbelief.

"Oh!" Damon said, suddenly putting together the pieces of the joke with a dimly understood cultural memory. Then, "*Oh!*" again. His eyes widened a bit, thinking about how that joke must have played to rooms full of strangers.

"After your mother died I tried all sorts of things. You saw that clown thing I did on Steve Allen. I was trying all sorts of bits," Alvie Grunman told his daughter.

"But . . . the holocaust?" Alice said.

"You don't make jokes out of tragedies," Simon said with certainty.

"Nonsense," Poppa said. Then he turned to Damon. "You listen to me, Damon." Damon listened. He listened as hard as he could and he did his best to commit what his grandfather said to memory. Poppa said, "We're Jews. We don't believe in tragedy. We believe in horror, atrocity and injustice. We just recognize that all of these are inherently hilarious."

Damon laughed.

Alice hissed a series of little hisses. Simon glared at Poppa for contradicting him but after a moment, maybe less, he snorted just a little bit. This was not a derisive snort. Something had actually caught him by surprise.

"There was something else I was gonna tell   you. What else was I gonna tell the kid?"

"I have no idea," Simon said. He turned the tip of his cigarette in the ashtray, contemplating a crossword clue.

Alice shrugged.

"Straight man," Damon said.

"Ah," Alvie Grunman said. "Straight man indeed. This is something you need to know. Straight man is hard. Straight man is as hard as funny. Maybe harder."

"Seriously?"

"Yeah. You gotta know how jokes work for straight man, but you gotta look like you don't. You gotta be able to look like a fool without ever feeling like a fool. People can laugh at someone who looks like a fool. But once the guy feels like a fool . . . then everyone just worries about him. You know what I mean?"

"Um," Damon said, which was less embarrassing than 'No.'

"Abbott, he could stand there, baffled, frustrated, unable to keep up with Costello's nonsense. He never needs to prove that he's smarter. We have to feel like he's smarter, but still the joke has to play and the joke is always about the other guy getting something wrong. Costello's always got the logic just a little bit off. That's where the real genius lies. Right? So Abbott, he's gotta be smarter and stupider at the same time. He has to be certain and confused all at once. Plus, he never gets to feel like he's the guy getting the laugh. It's a hard job, straight man."

"It doesn't look hard."

"Neither does funny if you do it right. If you do it right, everything looks easy, easy, easy. That's why civilians all think they can do it just as well as we can. We make it look like it's off the cuff. They believe us. We make it look like we're stupid. They believe us. Then they think, 'Hey, these idiots can be funny off the cuff. I'm smarter than them; I should be able to do that too.'"

"So, civilians can't be comics OR straight men?"

"Yep. But they're all pretty certain they can be either."

1977

"Lenny's absolutely a civilian," Damon told Poppa.

He tossed a chunk of bread out for a duck that had come close to the shore. The duck snatched it up, shook some water off of it and then swallowed it down.

"Yeah. Yeah, he is. So is Simon." Poppa said.

"Yeah. Yeah, he is."

"It's weird, 'cause your father's smart. He's creative. He loves comedy. He loves movies and books, but he doesn't get it."

"Yeah."

"Your mother . . . she could've been a great comic. She took after Trixie."

"Trixie was funny, huh?"

Poppa turned the heavy gold ring on his finger. He said nothing. He just looked out at the ducks for a long, silent moment. Then he said, "Your mother made a choice. I don't know when, and I don't know why. She decided she didn't want any part of it. Just shut down that whole part of her brain."

"Tell me about Grandma," Damon said.

Poppa took a long time before he answered. It wasn't as though he was looking for the right words or trying to control his emotions. It was far more as if he had to rifle through a huge rolodex of things he wanted to say and choose the right one. Or the right ones. After several slow, thoughtful breaths, he said, "The night that I met your grandmother, she said something so funny that I knew we were gonna do an act together. We met and we talked and we kissed and I said, 'Am I the first man you've ever loved?' and she said, 'Do you want my stock answer?' Then I laughed for forty-two years."

Damon looked out at the ducks and tried to imagine what forty-two years felt like. In his mind, that span of time had to be as heavy as his grandfather's ring.

1982

Damon sat down in the waiting room to think. He needed a few minutes to gather his thoughts before he left the hospital and faced the world again. The paper bag felt heavy in his grip.

He wondered if his grandfather could really be recovering as well as he claimed to be. He tried to imagine Poppa dying. He tried to imagine what it would be like to be the only one in his family who understood jokes, the only one who knew what it was to own a room, to pull the roaring laughter from the darkness.

Had the bag been less soggy from his sweating

palms it would have made crinkling noises as his hands shook. He sniffled and it was the first time he realized that he was crying. All the people around him distracted themselves from their life-or-death troubles and he was weeping like a baby over the dilemma presented by an old man's joke.

Damon did not want to be a part of the joke. It didn't seem funny to him. Nothing seemed funny to him. His grandfather was in a sterile hospital room, in over- starched sheets. He was making jokes about rectal probes and flirting with nurses and he looked a hundred and eighty-four years old. He might be dying and Damon could see nothing in it but tragedy.

He glanced up at the industrial-sized clock on the wall and his eye fell on the framed instructional poster just below it and to the left. The poster featured cartoonish illustrations of men with greenish-gray faces, thermometers in their mouths, ice-packs on their heads. It described symptoms they were experiencing. It explained in detail the difference between symptoms that indicated the flu and lesser symptoms indicating, according to the poster, "That one had simply caught a common cod."

Damon laughed aloud in the waiting room.

The other friends and family of patients looked at him, startled at the sound. He considered reassuring them that possibly, just possibly, their loved ones weren't sick at all, that perhaps they had just had a successful day fishing on Lake Chikatahooie.

He did not give in to the impulse. Still chuckling, he got up and left the hospital.

He took the brown paper bag with him. He knew now, with absolute certainty that he would keep the promise he had made. Whether Poppa died today   or tomorrow or ten years down the road, Damon would do what had been asked of him.

1985

"Damon!" the vaguely familiar voice of Andy Lebaron said over the phone, "I'm so glad you called me back. Listen, Lester Doheney told us about your Grandfather's passing and about . . . you know . . . what happened at the funeral."

Damon winced. He was quite certain at that moment that one more person was about to scold him for what he'd done. Never mind that it had been Poppa's idea, or that he had merely been keeping a promise he'd made years earlier. He'd been hearing about how wrong he'd been for days and he had begun to internalize the scolding voices. Now, anybody who mentioned the event was surely getting ready to launch into a tirade against him. At least over the phone he was unlikely to be punched. He said nothing.

"We're putting together sort of a tribute dinner down here at the Friars' on Friday night and we all thought it might be nice if you'd come down and be one of the speakers for us."

Damon let out a slow breath. He had only been on the Friars' Club stage once and that had been in the middle of the day with his Grandfather lecturing him on proper microphone use. "You know," he said, "I'm not actually a member of--"

"Yes, you are."

"What? No. I can't afford—"

"Alvie took care of that for you, kid. He was a life-time member and he used his discount to leave you a lifetime membership when he passed. He didn't tell you this?"

Damon was stunned. He felt a little bit dizzy. "And you want me to come speak at some sort of a memorial thing?"

"It's at the Friars' club, kid. So, you know. You better be as fuck-ass funny as Alvie says you are. Said you were. Said you are."

"Wait. Wait. Wait. Let me get a piece of paper. This Friday you said?"

"Yeah," Andy Lebaron said. "Dinner at eight. People start talking at eight thirty."

"Okay. Yeah. Um. How long am I doing?"

Andy Lebaron laughed a loose, open laugh. He said, "Alvie was right. You really are one of us."

2004

Damon tapped his head against the door behind him as he stroked the cat's throat with his thumb.

"Really, Damon?" Cynthia asked from inside. "Am I taking too long in here for you?"

Damon chuckled. "Sorry. No. I wasn't knocking to get in."

"Good. 'Cause I think there's still some food in me from the early eighties that I haven't purged yet."

"Do you think something's wrong? Should I call the doctor?"

"Yes, Damon. Please call the doctor and tell him that your wife has a parasite growing in her abdomen and it's making her puke."

"You mean like a tapeworm or something?"

"No, I mean a child, you idiot. This is what happens when you get pregnant."

Damon said, "I'm pretty sure when I get pregnant, there's a lot more media interest."

"Okay. Shut up and let me vomit now, okay?"

"Okay," Damon said, but it didn't stop him from sitting on the floor and worrying. "My father thought he just had heartburn."

"I'm not having a heart attack."

"My mother gave him Tums."

"I'm nauseated because I'm having a baby and it's screwing with me chemically."

"She still feels guilty about it," Damon said.

"I'm not going to die," Cynthia reassured him from inside the bathroom.

"Do you know how much longer I can carry guilt than my mother?"

"Do you have the slightest idea, Damon, how much this is not about you right now?"

Damon chuckled. "Yeah. But I forget. It's good that you remind me."

CHAPTER EIGHTEEN

2004

Damon ran to keep up with the nurses who wheeled Cynthia toward the delivery room. She lay on her back, sweating. There was nothing of the lovely glow of pregnancy about her now. Now she was a sweating, unhappy woman with a huge belly. She shouted, "Morphine! Demerol! Heroin! Morphine! Demerol! Heroin!"

"Does this mean she wants an epidural?" one of the nurses asked.

"I'm pretty sure—" Damon began.

"Are you fucking kidding me?" Cynthia interrupted. "What? Did you think that's just some demented Lamaze mantra? Maybe you're not aware of this, but there's a goddamned person trying to crawl through my twat!"

The nurse choked a bit. Damon had the sense that she was trying not to laugh at someone who was so obviously in pain.

Damon said, "'Twat'. You don't get a lot of 'twat' these days."

"You should really shut up now, Damon."

"Sorry. Sorry. Yes. You're right." He controlled the impulse to write jokes, to construct punch lines around everything he saw, everything he heard. This moment, he reminded himself for the four-thousandth time, was not about him.

Reaching a set of double doors, the nurses pushed Cynthia on through and kept Damon back.

"I thought I was going to be there when—"

"You will. Just wait here until we get her situated. Okay?"

"Okay," Damon said.

He let them go ahead without him. He was a little disappointed, a little let down in the suddenly silent hallway. He also felt a little bit of embarrassment as he realized that he secretly hoped they might forget to come get him when it was time. He was already a little bit dizzy, a little bit overwrought and worried.

He was self-conscious about the re-emergence of the Comedy Tourette's. He wanted to think that he was ready to pull away to make the delivery easier for Cynthia, but the truth was, he was afraid to be there, afraid he'd be in the way, afraid he'd faint, afraid he would blurt out inappropriate comments. He was afraid that when the pressure was really on, he would not be exactly the man he wanted to be.

1985

Damon stood at the back of the room, nervous, shuffling a bit on the worn carpet. He tried to identify the guests by the backs of their heads. He had seen some of them coming in. Milton Berle was there. Buddy Hackett. Dozens of faces he recognized but had no names for. Others whose acts he knew by heart. Carl Ballantine was there. Charlie Callus. They were all there for Poppa, to pay their respects, to say goodbye.

He was one of them. He hated himself for being excited about his membership to the club. He hated himself for being thrilled at the performance opportunity. He hated himself for having screwed up his grandfather's funeral for so many people. He loved that he was one of *these* people, though. He loved that these people had known his grandfather and that his grandfather had made him into one of them.

Big Joey Ptolemy stood at the microphone. He said, "Lady and gentlemen," and the room laughed. There were actually a few women present, but not many. Damon heard a laugh that he recognized as Rose Marie. A laugh that he recognized from television reruns he had watched as a child. "We got two more people who wanna say somethin' tonight and one of 'em's Steve Allen so that hardly even counts. He always wants to say somethin'." The room laughed. "The next guy coming up here to the stage . . . this kid . . . anyone ever talked to Alvie heard all about this kid. According to Alvie this kid is pretty much the second coming of Christ, only funnier. And that's saying something. A lotta you don't know this, but Jesus was a funny fuck. They talk about the trick with the fishes and loaves, the walking on water. But they don't talk about the guy's patter. He used to do a thing, he's turning water into wine, he's talkin' a mile a minute about Ernest and Julio Gallo, had the people pissing on their sandals."

The room groaned. It was a friendly groan that said, more than anything else, "Don't do your act. Bring the kid up already."

Big Joey was having none of it, though. He said, "Oh. That upsets you? You don't want me to talk about Jesus? 'Cause I'll go after President   Fuckin'

Reagan next, just to watch Hope pop an aneurysm. Swear to god, the guy's stumbling around the White House right now askin' secret service guys what his call time is for tomorrow."

A small laugh came, an uncomfortable groan.

"The truth make you all uncomfortable? Fine, I'll play the party line. Ronnie's in complete command of his faculties. He's getting together with FDR tomorrow for a game of tennis. Abe Lincoln was gonna play but he's gonna be out picking up chicks. I will round up your sacred cows and open a kosher steak house, you alteh cocker fucks."

The room exploded into laughter. People pounded on tables. Damon saw someone doubled over and for a moment he was afraid he was witnessing the last breath of a comedy legend.

Joey Ptolemy then did something that shocked Damon with its rightness, its beauty, its perfection. Just as the laughter peaked, he said, "This kid did something we all heard about. Only a few of us were there to witness it, but he gave Alvie the send-off he deserved. I don't know anybody who could have bigger balls than this guy has and you all just gotta give it up for him. He's the famous grandson, the boy we've all heard about for years. Damon Blazer!" And the fading laughter gave way to the end of the introduction and then the welcoming applause and Damon walked up onto the stage.

1982

"You know what the hardest part of comedy is, Damon?"

Damon was already halfway out the door when Poppa asked the question. He was ready to leave. The smell of the hospital was beginning to depress him. He had the brown paper bag. He had made the promise. He didn't know what more the old man could want of him. Was he really going to keep him in this little white room until one or the other of them died?

"Sorry," he said. "I missed it. Try it again."

Poppa chuckled. "No, kid. Not timing. That's the most *important*."

Damon nodded.

"You hear me say, 'What's the most *important* part of–'"

"Timing," Damon said.

"That's my boy. No. The *hardest* part. The hardest thing in the world. Getting off at the right time."

"Really? I get off when I see the light. Sometimes I go a little over, but generally it's–"

"No. That's now. At the beginning you got the light, you got the guy waving the candle at you. Whatever. No. Later. You're headlining, you're the big shot. Nobody's saying get off the stage. But you gotta do it. And you gotta do it at the moment when it feels wrong."

"When it feels wrong?"

"Yeah. If it's going bad, you're chasing the laugh,

it's over. Say thank you and get off the stage."

"Yeah?"

"Yeah. You wanna stay. You wanna win 'em back, prove you're better than they give you credit for. But it ain't gonna happen. You gotta let that go. And if it's going well, that's the really hard one. You been on a while, and suddenly there's a huge laugh, bigger than you've ever heard, you own 'em. Say thank you and get off the stage."

"What?"

"You get that kind of a laugh, it ain't climbing from there. You get out on a laugh whenever you can, Damon. Don't lose 'em again. You hear the explosion, you get out on a laugh. Hardest thing in the world, that one. You want that laugh to go on forever. You want it again, right away. You want more and more and more. But once you've heard it, once that room is popped, broken, you let it go. You'll have another chance another day. Don't fuck it up. Get off the stage. Right then. Right that moment."

Damon closed the door and moved back toward the plastic chair. Suddenly he wasn't ready to leave. Suddenly he felt there was too much to learn from the man for him to just walk out without absorbing all of it.

Poppa said, "Now get the hell out. I'm tired. You trying to kill me with all your damn questions?"

Damon chuckled. He left.

1985

Damon looked out at the roomful of candle-illuminated comedy luminaries. He moved to the microphone. He felt a clutching, closing feeling in his throat. He took a long, comfortable in breath. He said, "I never really knew Alvie Grunman."

The room chuckled.

"The man I knew was Poppa, my grandfather. I adored him."

He felt the discomfort in the room, the fear that he was going to betray them all, that he was going to be sentimental and earnest.

"Poppa was always deeply conflicted in his relationship with me," Damon went on. "On the one hand, he felt every grandfather's natural impulse to support and advise a beloved grandson. On the other hand, he felt every comic's natural impulse to undermine a vastly superior talent." The line took the room completely by surprise. The laughter came in three distinct waves and Damon rode them, reeling, looking out at this roomful of strangers all of whom he seemed to know so very, very well.

2004

Damon stood in the hallway for a long moment before wandering back toward the plastic chairs in the waiting room. Studying the pattern of the linoleum tiles as he walked, he realized that he had been

in this hospital before. He seemed to know these tiles
very, very well. He knew the smells and the feel of the
traction under his feet.

1994

"Rock it. Don't lift it," Matthew suggested.

"Either help or shut up," Damon replied. He tried
to lift the edge of the refrigerator onto the hand
truck.

"You want me to go with you?"

"Where?" Damon grunted, wrestling with the refrigerator. He had it halfway onto the flat plate of the
truck. A few more inches and he'd be ready to lean it
back and steer it through the door and down the
stairs to the rented U-Haul.

"To the east coast. To your dad's . . . thing."

"No, Matt. I don't need you at my father's funeral. Why would I want you at my father's funeral?"

"I'm just saying," Matthew said, chewing pizza.
"Your Dad's not gonna be there to moderate and you
are gonna be spending time with your brother."

Damon was not aware of any particular thought
crossing his mind just then, but he lost traction under his left foot and the huge appliance dropped the
inch or two he had lifted it, catching his finger under
its weight. He heard the sound of the bone snapping
even as he threw his weight forward to tilt the thing
away from him and pull his hand free in the second
he had before it fell back onto the hand truck.

"Jesus!" he shouted. "Crap." He looked at his
hand, at the finger bent at a bad, clearly   unhealthy

angle. He felt his mouth go dry and heard a strange buzzing sound as he said, "I think I need to go to a hospital. Do we know where there's a hospital?"

Cynthia said, "I'll drive. Matt, can you finish packing things up here, you think?"

"Should I come with you?"

"Finish packing," Cynthia said.

She led Damon out of the apartment and down the stairs to the car. As he walked, he said, "Lifting it was a mistake. I should've rocked it."

2004

Damon sat in a blue plastic chair and wondered which chair Cynthia had sat in while he got his finger reset ten years earlier. He realized that she would've been in an entirely different waiting room, that the emergency room was far, far away from this section of the hospital.

He wondered why it was taking so long to get her situated, taking so long for someone to come get him. He began to wonder if something had gone wrong, if there had been some sort of complication, how long it had been since he'd sat down. He won- dered what time it was and then realized that he was staring at a clock. He also realized he had no idea what time it had been when he sat down. He wondered why he had   suddenly lost all ability to gauge time.

1985

Damon knew he'd been on stage for about ten minutes and it had already been a long evening. He'd done all the jokes he'd written for the occasion and a few he hadn't planned on doing. He'd gotten some good laughs, but it didn't really feel like he was going to pop the room. He made a decision and pushed to the end of his prepared remarks.

"This is an important evening for me. I thank you all for it. Poppa would have been very pleased to see all of you here, to see this going on in his honor. I remember when I was about seventeen, I had just started doing comedy and Poppa had a heart attack. I went to visit him in the hospital and I asked him if he thought I was any good as a comic. He said, 'You're a funny boy, Damon.' It meant a lot to me, but I was very young and arrogant and self-certain. I said, 'I'm a man, Poppa.' And without missing a beat he said—"

As Damon spoke the words, he was stunned to hear the entire room speak the words with him as though they'd spent the whole day rehearsing to be in unison. Damon and two hundred old comics and comediennes all at the same time said, "You're not that funny." Laughter and applause filled the room.

Damon was dumbfounded. Had Poppa told them about this? Had he told every one of them about that moment? Had it been as important a moment to him as it was to Damon? Had he been as proud of the line as Damon had been impressed by it?

The long, loud response began to fade and Damon's heart sank. He wanted it back, the sound, the love, the roar of the room. He wanted more of it. For a half-second he thought that maybe he could pull some stuff from his act now, keep them going, keep it rolling. He suddenly understood why Poppa had described this as the hardest part, the most difficult element of the most difficult profession. He knew what he had to do and once he knew, there was no point in pretending he could do otherwise.

He said, "Thank you all very much," and the swelling applause as he left the stage told him he had done exactly the right thing. As he moved past Big Joey Ptolemy, the older man shook his hand firmly, leaned in toward him, grinned at him and muttered, "Pretending to share a private moment of conversation about your grandfather . . . big hug . . ." He hugged Damon, smelling of aftershave and performance sweat, and then moved past him to the microphone.

"And lastly, ladies and gentlemen, a man who is a treat to listen to any chance he's given, Mr. Steve Allen!" and the original host of *The Tonight Show* took the stage right after Damon Blazer.

2004

"Mr. Blazer?" a woman in green scrubs said.

"Yeah," he said.

"Come on in, now," the woman said. "But I want you to stay out of the doctor's way. So once I place you, I don't want you wandering up for a closer look. All right?"

"Sure," Damon said. As he said it, he stood up

much too fast and thought for a moment he was going to pass out on the floor of the waiting room. He
slowed his breathing and dropped to one knee for a
moment, just so that if he collapsed he wouldn't have
so far to fall. It was a trick that he'd learned years
earlier when he smoked pot all the time. Every now
and then a head rush would take him down suddenly. He'd learned to get low the moment he noticed the
blackness starting to close in.

To the nurse it seemed an odd moment of prayer.
Then he recovered and followed her toward the delivery room.

CHAPTER NINETEEN

2004

Damon stood near the door, one hand against the wall to steady himself. He wanted to be witnessing a miracle, to be filled with awe as his infant emerged into the light for the very first time, looked around at the strangers who ushered her into the air she would breathe for a lifetime and uttered her first sounds. The actual event though, upset him.

Cynthia cried out intermittently with pain and effort. Two nurses gave her instructions, when to breathe, when to push, when to wait a moment, as though that could ever be a good idea under circumstances like this. The doctor guided the slimy head out of his wife's body and her body opened up grotesquely wide to allow this to happen.

"Are you okay?" somebody asked. "You look a little pale."

Damon wanted to answer but he did not trust his own ability to form coherent words.

1985

Steve Allen made a few opening remarks. He cackled his trademark laugh. Then he said, "I pulled some footage from my archive at Meadowlane Productions."

"Of course you did," someone shouted. The room laughed.

Steve laughed again. He said, "Alvie made two appearances on my show. The first one was with Trixie. I don't think it's ever aired since that first time. At the risk of putting Damon through a Delmore Schwartz experience, can we run that, please?" He cackled his trademark laugh stepping back from the microphone so that the sound faded as abruptly as the lights.

The big video screen behind him on stage flicked to life and the stage lights dimmed around him.

Damon stiffened in his seat. There was footage. All this time there had been footage of his grandfather performing with Trixie and he had never known. He had never known to look for it, had never known to write a letter to Meadowlane Productions, to the Friars' Club. He had never known to ask Poppa about it. Had Poppa known that this was out there somewhere? Was there a reason he had never told Damon?

As the images on the screen brought the past into the present, Damon entirely forgot the mental note he had made moments earlier to look up Delmore Schwartz, to find out what that joke had meant.

On the screen Steve Allen was much younger. His hair seemed jet black, oiled. The image flickered, not quite as disruptively as kinescoped images would, but still, the quality was not modern videotape. The audio sounded tinny and distant as young Steve Allen said, "And so, without further ado or nearer adon't, please welcome to the stage Alvie Grunman and Trixie Dufresne." Applause that h a d faded decades ago came through the speakers as Poppa and the woman he loved moved up to the microphone.

Damon had never seen her before, this woman. Still, he knew her at once as his grandmother. He could see his mother in her. He could see Poppa's love for her in his eyes.

Poppa was a young man then, straight and clean-suited and stepping into a bright future. He said, "Trixie, have you ever seen such a terrific crowd?"

"I can't see them now, Alvie," she said.

"Lights too bright for you, darling? I can ask them to dim them for you."

"Aren't you sweet, Alvie! No. The problem isn't the lights, dear. It's just that I'm a broken typewriter."

"A broken typewriter? I don't understand."

"I only have eyes for you."

"Awww, Trixie. You say the sweetest things."

"I have to, Alvie. I never learned to bake."

As corny as the routine was, it sparkled with mutual adoration and the live audience at the Friars' Club watched with the timing of professionals, laughing and then going quiet fast enough to catch every line, to let Damon catch every line.

"Well tonight, you're cooking with gas, Baby!"

"Why thank you, Alvie," she said. "And that means, of course, that you will be playing the part of gas."

"Hey," Poppa said, seemingly startled. "Now wait a minute."

"Well, okay. But they've only given us five to begin with."

"I think we've already used up two and we haven't told any jokes yet."

"That can't be my fault. I didn't write the act."

The audience of long ago on the television laughed and clapped as did the audience in the room with Damon.

Alvie Grunman, thirty-five and frustrated, sighed.

"Tell me, Darling. Am I the first man you've ever loved?"

"Do you want my stock answer?"

The laughter was huge then, roaring. Alvie on the television had to pause, fiddling with his hands in his pockets, adjusting his cuff links while he waited for the laughter to die down.

"I suppose it was an arrogant question, Trixie. I don't know how you put up with me."

"You're a funny man, Alvie. I've always loved funny men."

"Darling. Will you marry me?"

Trixie looked at him, almost pityingly and said, "You're not that funny."

The room erupted into applause and laughter as young Steve Allen moved across the televised stage to shake Alvie's hand and old Steve Allen moved back to the microphone as the lights came back up on stage.

Damon sat in stunned silence at the back of the room. A straight man. Poppa had been her straight man. It had never occurred to him that this might be the relationship, that this might be how their act worked. Poppa had certainly never told him he'd been a straight man. It seemed inconceivable. Impossible. It seemed, somehow, unfair. How could he have been that man, always letting someone else get credit for the laugh, never taking it for himself?

1982

Poppa waved a pale, frail hand at Damon. He said, "You're stuck in a hospital bed like this, it doesn't matter. You think you might die, it doesn't matter. You think the worst thing in the world has happened to you, it doesn't matter, kid. You find the funny in it. You find the way to make people laugh. You're too choked up to talk, you do a pratfall. You're too broken to do a fall, you make a face. You understand me?"

"Yeah, Poppa. I understand you. But this—" He peered into the paper bag.

"This, Damon, is the stuff legends are made of!"

"You want this to be the legend they tell about you?"

"About me?! Fuck no, Damon. It's not funny if it's me. This is the legend they tell about you! You don't ever tell anybody this was my idea! Not ever! That's part of the promise. It has to be."

"Christ, Poppa. Do you know what you're asking me to do here?"

Poppa nodded at him. His eyes gleamed. He grinned as though he was looking out over the vast expanse of the future and it was filled with Trixie all over again.

1985

Steve Allen was speaking again and Damon forced his attention back onto the old man.

"A lot of you knew, after Trixie passed away, Alvie was a mess. He didn't know if he could be funny again on his own. Never mind the fact that he worked the circuit for—what—twenty some years before he met her? That didn't matter. He thought he was done. I got a call from Lester Doheney saying he was in trouble. Not Lester. Alvie. Lester was always in trouble. No. This was about Alvie. He wasn't going out. He wasn't doing shows. He wasn't writing anything. I called him and just told him he was booked on the show. I gave him a date and told him to show up with a funny act. I figured it would get him out of his apartment, force him to write something new, some jokes he could do on his own. On the day of taping, I had no idea what he would bring in. Let's take a look at that spot. Can we?"

The lights shifted once more to let the video flicker visibly.

The sound faded in sharply as Steve Allen said, "Mr. Alvie Grunman!" And the audience applauded.

The old, black-and-white footage brought Alvie up to the microphone in an overcoat and a hat. He nodded a brief bow to the crowd. He took off his hat, looked around for a place to put it, hung it on the microphone and then mouthed silently the words, "Good evening ladies and gentlemen."

The crowd laughed.

Startled by the lack of sound, Alvie tapped the hat, realized the problem and lifted it off the microphone. He looked around again for a place to put the hat.

Finding none, he lifted the mic out of the stand, placed the hat onto the mic stand and grinned at the crowd. He slipped his left arm out of his overcoat and then his right, pulling the microphone through the sleeve with it.

The audience, seeing the problem he'd created for himself, began to laugh again. Apparently unaware that he now had the mic cord running through the sleeve, he held the coat in one hand, the mic in the other and looked for a place to hang his coat. He moved toward Mr. Allen's desk but was pulled up short by the mic cord.

He went back to the mic stand, put the hat back on his head, put the mic back in the cradle and turned to walk the coat over to the desk.

The coat with the cord through it pulled the mic stand off balance. With the grace of Fred Astaire working a coat rack, he circled elegantly, righting the stand with his foot.

He examined the cord, the mic, the coat, the stand. He stood still, seemingly doing nothing at all and yet it was absolutely clear that he was slowly sorting out the dilemma. He tugged on the coat once and pulled the stand sharply off balance whacking himself in the forehead with the microphone with a resounding thump.

The audience howled.

Alvie glared at them. They laughed harder.

He pulled the coat up the cord and down over the mic until the stand itself had passed through the

LAUGHS LAST | 195

sleeve. Now the coat was worn by the microphone stand instead of by the cord, with the one sleeve completely inside out. It pooled around the base of the stand, the free sleeve trailing off toward the back of the stage.

Giving up on that problem, Alvie stepped up to the mic but before he could speak, his right foot hit the trailing sleeve and he did a stunning backward pratfall. He seemed to bounce back to his feet and straightened his cuffs, a futile attempt to look unfazed. He glared at the coat sleeve. He glared at the laughing crowd. He took off his hat and threw it to the ground in a rage.

He reclaimed his composure.

He picked up the hat, dusted it off, placed it over the microphone, stepped up and again, mouthed a silent greeting as his foot slipped again on the sleeve. He sighed, lifted the coat, found it impossible to clear over the microphone with the hat there, took the hat off the mic, put it back on his head, lifted the mic out of the stand, put the hat back on the stand. He put his arm into the wrong end of the inside-out sleeve, and then followed it down until he lay on the floor and could slip his other arm into the right end of the trailing sleeve. He shifted onto his back and pushed the mic stand free of his coat sleeve from the inside, tossed his hat into the air, rolled to his feet, dropped the microphone back into the cradle as the hat landed squarely on his head and stood, center stage, behind the mic exactly as he had been on his entrance. He said, "Good evening ladies and gentlemen," and the music swelled, indicating that his time was up.

Young Steve Allen, laughing with glee, moved across the stage toward him saying, "Alvie Grunman, ladies and gentlemen. The great Alvie Grunman."

The crowd on the television and the crowd in the room both exploded into applause. As the picture faded, young Steve Allen shook Poppa's hand and Poppa whispered something to him.

Old Steve Allen returned to the microphone in the Friars' Club. He said, "Alvie—I don't know if you could see that he was whispering to me there—he said to me, 'I'm sorry I didn't have jokes for you. I wasn't sure I'd be able to speak without crying over Trixie.'"

2004

As the tiny girl was placed on Cynthia's chest, the doctor and nurses moved in close to clean her with damp wash cloths. The incredibly small person made incredibly small gurgling noises, but they did not sound like unhappy gurgling noises.

Damon moved to Cynthia's side. He stroked her sweat-soaked hair, moved it out of her eyes and stared at the person they had collaborated to create.

"Name?" asked a woman in scrubs with a clipboard.

"Damon," Damon said.

"Lydia," Cynthia said.

Damon said, "What?"

Cynthia said, "They know our names. They've taken down all our insurance information and they've been talking to us. They want the kid's name."

"Oh. Yeah. She's Lydia. At least I think she is.

Was she carrying any ID when she came out?"

The nurse laughed. Cynthia sighed.

"Sorry," Damon said.

"It's okay. I'm sorry I called you an idiot," Cynthia said.

"When did you call me an idiot?"

"I may not have said it aloud."

"Ah."

CHAPTER TWENTY

2009

Lydia sat at the table between Damon and Alice. Cynthia sat to his right and Lenny sat opposite him. Tomorrow everyone would be showing up for the big Thanksgiving dinner, but tonight it was just the immediate family.

Damon's Mom put asparagus on Lydia's plate using metal tongs.

"Asparagus!" Lydia announced.

"That's right!" Alice said. "Does your Mom make asparagus at home?"

"She does! And I like it. And not just because it makes my pee smell funny."

Alice chuckled. "No. Not *just* because of that?"

"Nope. I also like the way it tastes."

Lenny shook his head. "That's a helluva kid you got there, Damon."

"Um. Thanks?" Damon asked, uncertain.

"She told me earlier that she loves F. Murray Abraham."

"M. Furry Abraham," Lydia corrected.

Lenny ignored her. "Does that seem odd to you? I mean from a five-year-old?"

"Not really," Damon said.

"He's been sleeping with her since she was an infant," Cynthia added.

Alice chuckled, serving herself mashed potatoes.

Lenny looked shocked. Shocked and troubled.

Lydia said, "His whiskers are all tickly."

2004

Damon stood in the darkness holding the infant in his arms. He rocked gently, shifting from one foot to the other. He felt the warmth and the weight of the little body against his chest, heard the small snoring sounds. He dared not set her down again. Cynthia needed sleep and Lydia kept crying whenever he tried to tuck her back into her crib.

He stood, rocking gently, and looked out through the window at the Los Angeles night.

"I'm going to try to be a good dad for you," he told the little girl in his arms. "At the very least, I'm going to try not to be a complete asshole."

1985

Damon walked with his family back toward the parking lot. The workers had stamped down the sod over the gravesite and the whole awkward crowd moved across the lawn now, heading back to their cars.

Lenny walked very close to Damon hissing accusations at him. "You're such an asshole. I don't know how you could do something like that. I don't understand what's wrong with you."

Damon did not tell him that he had made a promise, that it had been Poppa's idea. He shrugged and said, "I thought it was funny."

"Stop saying that," Lenny said.

2004

Damon thought about what he had just told his daughter. He said, "I'll try not to look for laughs at inappropriate times. I'll try not to embarrass you. I'll do my best." Then he added, "I can't make any promises though."

1985

Damon got out of the car and moved as quickly as he could into the synagogue. He blew past the Rabbi and the Cantor greeting mourners at the door, gathering them up for the viewing of the body. He made his way to the casket in his dark suit, clutching the brown paper bag in his nervous hand.

He leaned over the coffin. Poppa's face was made up to look only slightly less dead than it would have looked without the make-up. The skin at Poppa's cheeks seemed to hang back toward the pillow as though he was more affected by gravity, now that his spirit had left him. "All right, Poppa. I'm doing this 'cause I promised. I love you. Loved you. And I'm only doing this for you. You know that. Right?"

He waited for a moment as though Poppa might automatically feed him a straight line. He realized he had no punch line to respond with if it happened.

He pulled the prop from the bag, the plastic,

black-framed glasses with the silly nose attached, the bushy moustache and eyebrows. He pulled out the tiny tube, and he did what had been asked of him. Once everything was in place, all set, he kissed his fingertips, touched them to Poppa's forehead and stepped away from the casket. He sat at the back of the room. The Rabbi came in and sat down beside him. He said, "Are you ready, Son?"

"What?" Damon asked.

"Your grandfather told me a long time ago, when this day came you were to get a minute alone with his body before anyone else came in."

"You're kidding me."

"I'm not," the Rabbi said, but Damon imagined Poppa saying, "No. When I kid you, there will be humor content."

"Wow," Damon said. "He was that certain?"

"I don't know what that means," the Rabbi told him.

"I'm ready," Damon said.

The Rabbi nodded and let the mourners enter the room.

They formed a line that ran up the aisle to the left, the people who had loved Poppa, who had come to say goodbye. Many of them were old, and many of them were people Damon had never met, friends, colleagues. Among them were faces Damon recognized from television, mostly from the television of his childhood, The Tonight Show with Johnny Carson, The Smothers Brothers Show, Sonny and Cher. He fought the urge to use his grandfather's funeral as a networking opportunity. He fought the urge to behave like a fan.

The first of the mourners reached the casket.

They looked inside. The sniffling, shuffling feel in the room began to shift. As their eyes fell upon the man who had spent his lifetime making people laugh, a new sound struggled to emerge. The sight of him, dead and clowning, done up in funny nose and glasses, added a choking undertone of chuckles to the proceedings.

One after another, members of the family, the extended family, and Poppa's working family moved past the body and felt their mood shift instantly from one of sorrow to one of sheer, startled joy.

Simon, Damon's father, looked into the casket and then looked up sharply. His eyes found Damon at the back of the room. His eyebrows lowered sternly for a moment. Then Lenny moved forward, saw Poppa's face and gasped. He started angrily up the open right-hand aisle toward his younger brother at once. He had felt no grief to begin with. He had never been all that close to Poppa. To him, the whole day was already an irritating waste, dressing up, going to a service, a burial. Now this? It was too much. If he was forced to be here, to act respectful, what gave Damon the right to mess around? Mom had been crying all morning. Now she was going to have to see this?

Damon was aware of Lenny coming toward him, but he also saw a tiny older woman move toward the casket, a woman he recognized from Thanksgiving dinners long ago. Damon's miniature Aunt Sadie looked in then leaned toward the body. Then she said, "Eeeeep!" It was a high-pitched sound, startled, but also delighted. The sound caused her to laugh outright and at that moment it was as though the cork had been popped and the champagne was free. Laughter bubbled out of every throat that had been past the body. Even those who were still to come began to chuckle in reflexive emotional sympathy.

It had worked. It had been exactly as Poppa had said it would be. Every beat of the joke had played out and Damon could not have been more pleased with it at that moment had he written it himself.

He hated to take credit for it, hated that he had promised his grandfather that nobody would ever know that this moment was Poppa's, not his. This was the exact joke that Poppa wanted it to be. This was the joke that would change the way these people thought about funerals forever. It would change the way they thought about Alvie Grunman. It would change the way they thought about Damon.

1982

"I understand the idea, Poppa. But . . . crazy glue? Are you sure?"

"Damon. Listen. That's what makes it brilliant. You put the funny glasses on me, that's one thing. That's fine. But you *know* someone's just gonna take them off and then the whole thing goes to shit. No. You put them on and you use the crazy glue, now you got something. Do you remember your Great Aunt Sadie?"

"Vaguely. Used to come to Thanksgivings. Yeah?"

"Yeah. Tiny little old lady. Very funny. But also very traditional. She sees the glasses on me, I guarantee you she tries to take them off. But when she pulls on them and it's like I start to sit up with 'em? Oh, kid, that'll be something.

"She'll let out that little scream of hers. She'll say 'Eeeeep!' in that little old lady voice and then it'll be all over. I'm telling you, Damon. You gotta do the whole thing. You don't just set 'em on my face. You gotta glue 'em down. You have to promise."

"All right," Damon said. "All right, you crazy old fuck. I promise."

"That's my boy, Damon. That's all I ask."

1985

Lenny grabbed Damon by the arm and pulled him from the hard wooden bench. He dragged him, his fingers pressing into the younger man's muscles, back toward the exit and out into the chill air.

"What's your problem?" Damon asked, but he already knew the answer.

"You incredible asshole," Lenny said. "What is wrong with you? Huh? What the fuck is wrong with you? This is a funeral for God's sake. Have some— for fuck's sake, man. Have some respect. Why would you do something like that?"

Damon shrugged. "I thought it was funny."

2004

Rocking Lydia in his arms, Damon knew he would eventually embarrass her. Eventually all parents embarrass their children. All siblings embarrassone another. All husbands embarrass their wives and are embarrassed in return.

He also knew, with absolute certainty, that nothing Lydia did would ever embarrass him. He had known her for a little less than two weeks and already he could tell that this little person could simply do nothing wrong.

2009

Lenny poked at the food on his plate with his fork. The anger bubbled up slowly and finally he could stand it no longer. He said, "I don't think that's funny."

"Yeah," Damon said. "That happens with you."

"Seriously, Damon? Pedophilia?"

"M. Furry Abraham is our cat, Lenny. Relax."

"Why would you name a cat F. Murray Abraham?"

"M. Furry Abraham," Lydia corrected.

Lenny ignored her.

"Simmer down, Lenny," Alice said. "What do you care what they name their cat?"

"They only do it to make everybody else look stupid, Mom. You know that. Then I sit here getting all worried about Lydia and whatnot and it turns out they're just fucking with my head."

"Hey," Mom said. "Watch your language."

Lydia and Damon said, "English. Watch yours?"

Cynthia laughed. Alice hissed.

Lenny glared. "Great," he said. "Now you're making her into one, too?"

"Lenny," Alice said, but it sounded like a warning shot.

Lydia picked up an asparagus spear with her fingers. She used it to conduct an imaginary orchestra. Cynthia shook her head a tiny bit at her daughter and the girl ate the asparagus.

"What, Mom. What? Seriously. You want another one of these? After the way Damon screwed up your father's funeral?"

"He didn't, Honey."

"What are you talking about? People were laughing. Your dad was dead and people were laughing."

"It was the right thing to do. At the time . . . your father wouldn't have understood. I couldn't explain it to him. But my father . . . I think it's what he would have wanted, frankly. I think Damon got that one right."

"Right? How did he get that right?" Lenny asked, incredulous.

Lydia knew what they were discussing. She had heard the story. It was her favorite kind of story. Her mother and father had both told it to her many times and earlier in the day her grandmother had told it to her. They had all told it differently, but none of them was able to get through it without cracking up. Regardless of who told it, the real point was clear, the bit that was important, the bit that was exactly what her great grandfather would have wanted her to remember.

"I don't know what you're so upset about, Uncle Lenny," she said.

"You don't know what happened, kiddo," Lenny said.

"Poppa got out on a laugh. Didn't he?"

"What?" Lenny said.

"That's right, kiddo," Damon told his daughter. "Poppa got out on a laugh."

END

Author Bio

Dylan Brody is a humorist and storyteller. His five CDs, all released by Stand Up! Records can be found at amazon.com and iTunes, he has also released two full length digital downloadables through Rooftop Comedy/ Media. He lives and writes in Sylmar, CA where he shares a home with his two dogs, Sir Corwin the Beautiful Dog-faced Dog, Brindled Beast of Sylmar, Lord Buckley Sweetlips, Greatest of All Dane Mutts (the Dinosaur Slaying Dog), and his lovely wife whose name escapes him at the moment.

69439186R00120

Made in the USA
Columbia, SC
20 April 2017